The Empire of Arkania

The Avat Prince

VOLUME SIX

Cartography brushes used in map artwork designed by Joel Pigou
https://www.gumroad.com/joelpigou

ISBN 9781957330105

First Edition Printed April 2021
MVP TV Edition Printed July 2024

Printed by IngramSpark in the USA.

House MVP
16 Thomas Patten Dr., P.O. Box 21
Randolph, MA, 02368

https://www.housemvpmedia.com

The text of this book is set in 12-point Adobe Garamond Pro.

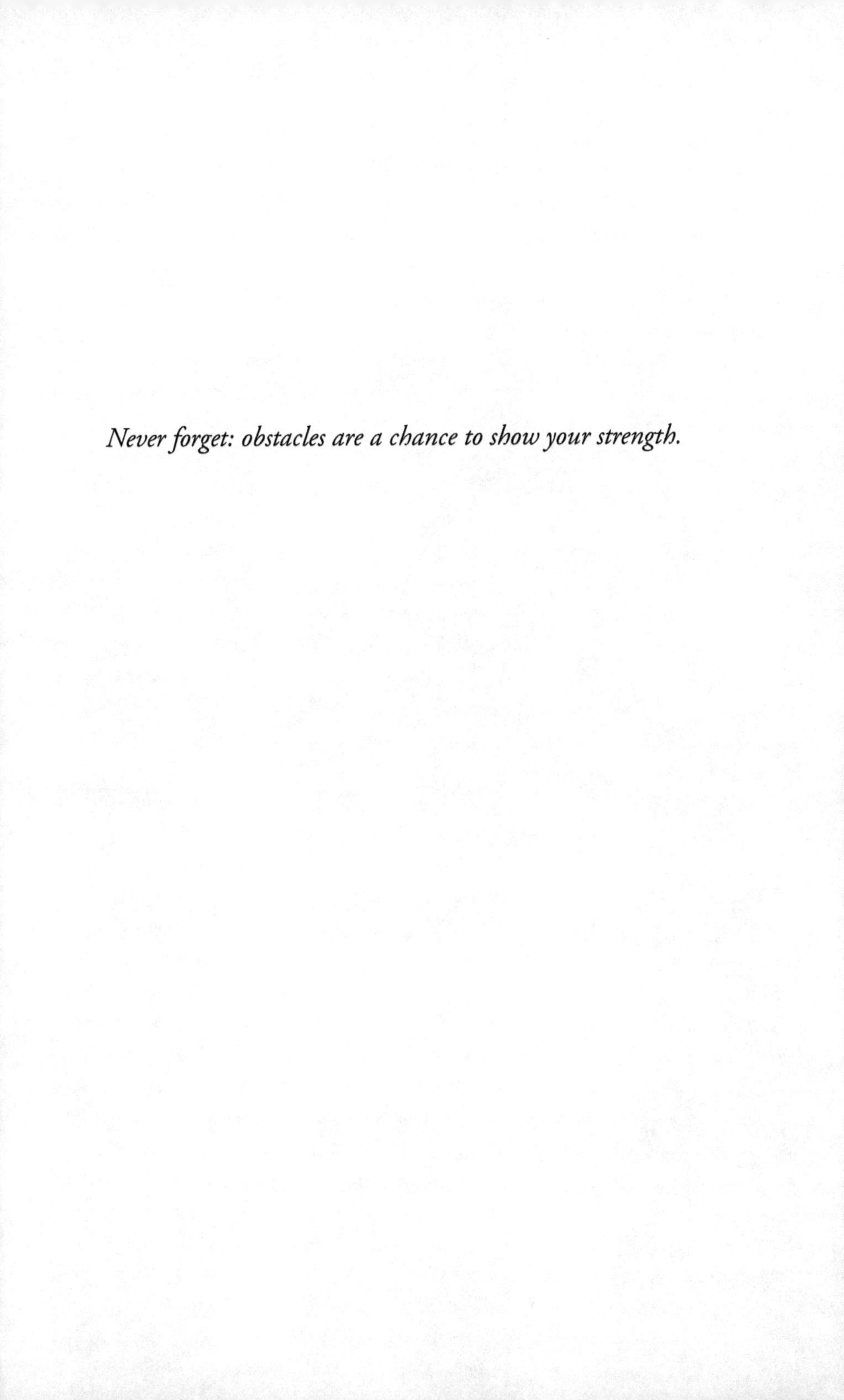

Never forget: obstacles are a chance to show your strength.

The Avat Prince

VOLUME SIX

WRITTEN AND ILLUSTRATED BY

MYRANDA V. PETERSON

TALES OF ARKANIA

To access locked skits for
THE AVAT PRINCE:

First, get reading!

When you see the word 'TV' at the end of a
sentence, it's time for a skit!

Illustrations are paired off with these pages.
Scan an illustration's QR code to access its skit.

Enter the password.

Enjoy the show!

(Don't forget to come back to keep reading the story!)

TV
MVP

HOUSE MVP

Previously in *The Avat Prince*...

One year after joining Taranis' auction raiders, Brent has become one of the village's best warriors. Liam has climbed the ranks alongside him, and Aaron has already made the same headway. Together, they form Taranis' most revered team of raiders.

Shortly after completing a mission that brought them all the way to the Liberation Front of Dukaris in Lenora Province, a black-clad stranger entered their camp at midnight. Sharing nothing about himself, the stranger showed an interest in Brent. He even knew about the Liberation Fronts, and claimed that Brent was chosen by something called Çaru'qu to stand against a global catastrophe, one that eclipses the Empire's racial tyranny. As for the details he didn't explain them, only saying that Chief Ivan could tell them more. Better yet the Elder, an enigmatic figure that Brent's only ever heard of in passing, has a daughter in Taranis who could do the same. After this, he disappeared in an aetherial windstorm of terrifying power.

Chief Ivan increased village security in case this stranger were to appear again. But Brent and Liam worry that Taranis is no match for him. Brent also inquired about Ivan's knowledge pertaining to Çaru'qu, and the chief explained that there are legends about the creature that speak of him in the same breath as the imperial gods Empyrean and Vedrah. But, the Empire doesn't recognize Çaru'qu as a deity, nor does it acknowledge his alleged power. That ends Ivan's response, but Brent suspects that he knows more.

Meanwhile, Emperor Koberius has launched a secret project that involves testing a drug that can enhance someone's quintessence. Elsewhere, a masked swordsman has slain the noble house of Lord Elkiah, a Lyrikan aristocrat. His motives are unclear, but deadly.

At the same time, Renée struggles to prove to her mother that she's worthy of joining Taranis' raiding forces, despite the lethal dangers that are clearly mounting in Arkania...

42

WRITHING NOISILY, BRENT *struggled with all the might of a six-year-old boy as he was dragged down the hall.*

"Stop!" he shouted, twisting and kicking, but the grip that the soldiers had on him was iron. "Let me go! No! Let go!"

The soldiers didn't speak. They only kept walking, filling his pointed ears with the shuffle of their armor as they marched down the hall.

"Let go!" Brent shouted again and he twisted his neck, aiming to get a glimpse of freedom behind him.

The other end of the corridor led to an atrium in Lyrik Estate, and the sunlight that fell into it had formed a halo around the figure standing there.

It was the viceroy of Lyrik Province: Diomedes Arkania.

"Father!" Brent shouted and he tried to break away from the soldiers again, but to no avail. "Father! What's going on? Where are they taking me?!" He wriggled and thrashed again, but it was still no use. "Father! Please! Help me!"

"Goblins belong in cages, boy." Diomedes' golden stare was hard and unfeeling. "Not dining with members of the imperial court."

Brent's face blanched.

Then his eyebrows knotted and he bit the hand of one of the guards that held him.

The man yelped, releasing him, and as soon as he did Brent kicked the knee of the other.

His grip, too, went lax, just enough for Brent to rip his arm free and run back to Diomedes.

The viceroy didn't even flinch as he approached, and he towered over the child when he came near.

He was not unlike a resplendent deity in his own right, with his even, brown skin and gleaming, golden eyes. His tunic and robes even glowed in the daylight, and his sandals were dressed with painted fili-gree. As for his face, it was sculpted with features that could make most women swoon, and a jawline that could make most men scowl with jealousy.

Brent tripped on his way to him, stumbled, and caught the front of Diomedes' robes for balance. Though he himself wore a rich, creamy tunic that was hemmed with patterns of red and silver, he couldn't at all compare to the wealth and masculinity of his father.

"Please don't let them take me!" he begged, staring into the man's empty expression. He could already hear the soldiers hustling towards him. "I'll be good! I promise!"

It was at that point that the soldiers reached him, and they snatched him up by the arms again. Their combined strength lifted him off the floor.

Grunting, he threw pleading eyes back to his parent. "Father —!"

His voice broke when Diomedes struck him across the face.

Stunned into silence, Brent allowed his head to hang there, with his eyes wide in shock. Something wet stung their corners.

"Know your place," Diomedes told him and, slowly, frightfully, Brent raised his head towards him. "My firstborn, a gift…only to become an abomination."

With that, Diomedes snatched the boy by the chin and turned his head, revealing one of his pointed ears.

"I once wondered if this was a malady. For the traits of a devil to appear in the seed of an Arkanian long after birth." His eyes narrowed. "To think that it would even infect you…although, perhaps it would explain what occurred during your aether training. Even it rejects you."

"I'm not…" Diomedes released him, and Brent's eyes welled up. When he lifted his head to the viceroy, he looked haunted and lost. "I didn't…"

Diomedes' own eyes creased, if only for a second, and there came the shortest glimpse of something that welled within his own heart. He seemed to be in pain, Brent thought, but then he recognized the emotion fully:

It was disappointment.

Pain…for disappointment.

"Take it to the basement," Diomedes decided, "before Viceroy Atticus and Prince Antony arrive. We don't need to create a scene."

"Yes, my lord."

"Fath…Father!" Brent gasped, and the soldiers again carried him off. Any resistance that he made was futile. "No, wait! I wanted to…" He struggled. "Let me go with you! Father! Father!*"*

"You are not to call me by that name." Diomedes turned away and started back through the atrium. "As of this moment, I have no son. I will not recognize a devil as my heir."

Brent relented at that, his body going slack as his father's rejection sank in.

Devil.

That's what people in the estate, and others in the city, called Avats sometimes. That name was even thrown out to the slaves who worked in the manor itself.

More insults came along with it: goblin. Gremlin. Creature.

An "it".

His shoulders sank, and his will to fight receded as the soldiers carried him away, into shadow, where the light couldn't reach…

It wasn't his fault, he told himself. It wasn't his fault that his ears had extended and sharpened over the last few months. It wasn't his fault that he could hear things most people couldn't. It wasn't his fault that the aether had exploded right in front of him, denying him access to it.

It wasn't his fault.

It wasn't his fault…!

He trembled and his voice broke out of him once again:

"FATHER!" he screamed.

But Diomedes didn't look back.

Only the swinging of the door at the end of the hallway answered Brent's call. Then at once he was pulled through, and dragged into shadow eternal.

He slammed his eyes shut —

And snapped up in bed in the present, his breath short.

He sat there for a moment, just breathing. At last, he looked around.

He was in his room.

Of course.

Just his room.

The first rays of dawn were beginning to peek through the window at his back. They caught some of the decorative masks that were hung up on the wall opposite him — mementos from when he'd participated in plays at the Feasts of Liberty when he was a boy — as well as the crate of knickknacks that was just below them.

All sorts of things filled it, ranging from maps of the valley to piles of detailed notes about the slave traders' movements that he himself had written. There were also a few gadgets that Harver had given him to test over the years, some of which had turned out to be duds that he'd never gotten around to returning. He probably never would.

What the light was able to illuminate the most, however, was on the wall right in front of him. It was a large map of the Empire, which Brent had copied while he'd still been a trainee. Ringing the Province of Lyrik were separate sketches that described certain areas in greater detail, and threads connected them to their corresponding locations in the Empire.

One of the drawings stood out to him at that moment. It was the most polished illustration, depicting a cabin out in the open fields with a barn not far behind it.

Adelle's home.

He sighed.

He'd thought of it, and of her, often, even now. Yet, for some reason, he still found himself dreaming about a different place: one that had barely served him the same level of care and compassion that she had. One that, truly, he wished he could forget.

Closing his hand into a fist, he leaned his arm over his knee and loosed one more quiet breath.

Some things just didn't change.

"I had been thinking about it. Trent's no scout, but he's not wrong about talk of war in Brusseir. Hard to say if things really are any different from how they've always been, but…" Aaron looked up from the ground and, hence, his pool of thought. "I wonder."

It was still early and so the village roads were empty, leaving a thin layer of mist to slither between the houses alone. A couple of paths away the stream burbled and every now and again, the sharp chirp of a bird pierced the quiet.

Only a moment ago Brent and Aaron had left their house and stepped into this pale, misty morn, both fully equipped for another raid. A few days had passed since they'd returned from their last mission in the Southern Mines and, as of the day before, they'd been informed of several new targets that were wandering into Taranis' field of operation. With there being more than one, a matching number of teams were being dispatched to handle them all.

But the timetables were different. As it happened, Brent, Aaron and Liam had been called upon to tackle the slave traders that would be arriving the earliest.

Brent had been disappointed at first. Despite his success rate he was never too keen on having such short breaks between assignments. But if it meant saving just one more Avat, he'd do it.

Aaron had awoken not long after he had, and so the two had set out for the Main House's conference room together, which had become a custom ever since Brent had joined Taranis' auction raiders. Liam on the other hand, had probably beaten them there — that, too, had become customary.

On the way, Aaron had brought up a certain topic that had apparently been nagging him since their return from Lenora. Centered around rumors of war that were circulating out of Brusseir Province, he'd been considering different instances of when he'd overheard related news during his own scouting missions.

"Typically, whenever the Katruskik tribes get restless, there are raids and roadside ambushes that are led by a radical who's never around for too long," the redhead explained as he and Brent carried on down the slope that led straight from their home to the Main House. "Last I heard, things have been getting intense: the rebels bombed Almstead a few weeks back."

"That's the second-biggest city up there, right next to the capital," Brent recalled, flabbergasted. "It's a fortress. They *bombed* it?"

"From what I heard," Aaron repeated. "Given what Trent said about that new alliance, they're probably the group that did it. I checked with some of our scouts the other day, and that stuff about Empyrean's Guard is also true.

"I'm worried. For the Liberation Front of Aerabis." His bright eyes narrowed. "Their exact location's a secret, even to us. But if things up there keep escalating they'll end up getting dragged into it."

"The chief there is your uncle, isn't he?"

"Yeah."

"You ever meet him?"

"Mom says I did, when I was little. But I hardly remember."

"Hm." Brent looked at the path ahead. "Haven't heard Pops talk about him much."

"It's not like they're pen pals. Doubt they've seen each other in years, with everything that's been going on. On top of that, he probably doesn't want anyone to think he's worried. He's the chief. And Taranis' foundation. If he falls apart, we all fall apart.

"Still, Uncle Aerie is his brother. Dad's probably the most worried about him out of everyone. He's already put out because he can't go on raids anymore and so, knowing that he might not be able to help if something happens to his only brother..." Aaron scowled. "That's gotta put a damper on your fighting spirit."

"Yeah...reminds me of how I kinda wish I had Pops around when I first started out." Brent laced his hands behind his head, still a little bothered that his guardian hadn't been there when he'd defeated his first slave trader. "He came on your first raid, didn't he?"

"Yeah. But what with the number of raiders, and sister villages, that we've since lost to Empyrean's Guard between then and now, we can't just send the chief up to the frontlines anymore. 'Specially when there's a chance that he could get captured, too. The head council's pretty much put their foot down about it."

Brent scoffed. "Like Pops'd ever get caught."

Aaron shrugged. "Dad's gotta keep things stable here at home. Don't think I like the idea of risking his safety either, to be honest. We've lost a lot of good people and as much as I hate to admit it, he's no less invincible than they were." The light in his eyes seemed to dim at that, as if the reality of his father's mortality had just now chipped off another piece of his ambitious ego.

In the two years that had passed since he'd become an official auction raider, Brent had noticed that that happened to Aaron a lot, as if the sobering realities of the world beyond Taranis were causing him to take things a lot more seriously than he used to. While he was still the same person that Brent and his friends had known since childhood, there could be no denying the fact that over the course of the past couple of years, he'd matured greatly.

Still, he wasn't the only one who was affected by the idea of Ivan not being invincible. Brent, too, felt the heaviness of this grave reminder, made known by the folds that formed between his brows as he turned his gaze away.

For the entire time that he'd been in Taranis, the village chief had towered over him in greatness and in size. Even now, part of him still thought that the chances of someone defeating him were slim to none.

Nevertheless, he supposed he couldn't entirely rule out the possibility. After all, a number of their best raiders had been outdone by slave traders. Who was to say that the same couldn't happen to Ivan?

As if he'd sensed the gloom that his own words had brought upon them, Aaron suddenly straightened up with a clearing of his throat. "'Sides, if anything happened to my old man, all of his responsibilities'd fall onto me. There's no way I'm ready for that."

At that, the solemn cloud evaporated enough for a smile to break through Brent's expression. "Yeah, no kidding," he laughed. "'Chief Aaron' doesn't even have a nice ring to it."

"Better than 'Chief Brent'," Aaron returned.

Brent looked up, considering. Then, he smiled to himself in a cocky sort of way.

Aaron noticed. "Wipe that grin off your face. You look like an idiot."

Brent toppled out of his fantasy. "Hey!"

"Anyway, I was just thinking out loud." Aaron hopped up the steps leading to the Main House's front doors. "Hopefully it doesn't get as bad as everyone thinks…"

Brent waited on the top step as Aaron reached for one of the handles. The older raider seemed to hesitate for a second.

Then, he shook his head and ultimately shook off whatever was dogging him. "Either way, we just need to focus on freeing the slaves for now."

"Not like I ever thought to do anything else," Brent said.

"Of course not, you're too simple." Aaron pulled the Main House's doors open.

"Shove it, *iytamhal*," Brent countered, adding the nickname in Katruskan.

"I told you to stop calling me mop-top!" Aaron returned fluently.

"Then get a haircut!" Brent parried in the same tongue.

Aaron groaned.

When they entered the building, they learned that the dining hall was silent. Not even the kitchens were awake for the preparation of breakfast.

Passing through the open hall, with its bench tables and sunbeams filtering through the windows, Brent and Aaron ascended to the second floor and approached the doors to the conference room. As they neared it, they overheard low voices coming from the other side. It seemed that, as they'd expected, some of the other raiders had already arrived.

Again Aaron reached the doors first and entered the room beyond. Brent walked in after him.

Jeffrey and Ivan were already there, as was Ben, Renée and Mekial's father. He was growing out his beard, which was now an even layer of stubble that covered his square jaw, and his dark eyes contained a certain childlike energy that, to this day, complemented his wife's more stern character. He'd retained his musculature thanks to his steady commitment to raiding, with two large arms that broke out of his sleeveless tunic, and his signature, curved sword was belted to his back. A set of knives hung from his belt as his secondary tools of warfare.

A couple of other raiders were also present: there was Eve, a brunette Avat who was also the mother of Dillon, one of the many village children who'd taken a liking to Brent and his friends; there was also a man named Rufus, a dark-haired and round-eared villager who lived a couple of houses away from Brent and Aaron with his wife and three children.

Tyre and Kro were also present, having made themselves comfortable against the opposite wall.

Tyre was in the middle of examining his bangs, but he looked up when Brent and Aaron came in.

Kro did the same, his hands held in front of his chest as he caused several beads to revolve rapidly between his palms. It was probably an aetherial training exercise.

"Good! You are here!" Ivan exclaimed almost as soon as he laid eyes on the new arrivals. He was standing at the head of the table.

"Then, all who's left is Liam," Jeffrey said, his place being directly opposite Brent and Aaron. "Strange of him to be last."

Brent did a double-take around the room. "You mean we actually beat him here?"

As if on cue the door opened again and Liam himself walked in, curved broadsword strapped to the back of his waist and a foggy look in his eyes. He appeared to be frowning through it.

"Sorry." He moved in so as to close the door. "Late night."

"Excitement kept you up?" Brent guessed, smiling.

"No. Eklaire gave us some of her mom's Arkanian prune pie yesterday. Lilian snuck some last night and wouldn't sleep." Liam joined him and Aaron beside the table. "Arkanian prunes make her hyper."

"Oh, yeah."

"All right, that's everyone. Let's begin." Jeffrey pulled a map out of a slot beneath the table and spread it out in front of everyone.

Together, those in the room gathered to get a better view.

Liam squinted.

Tyre noticed and he elbowed Kro. It took a second for the older sibling to figure out what the problem was before he understood to wave his arm, causing the lamps around the room to burn just a bit brighter.

The harsh frown on Liam's face eased up just a little. He glanced up and around, then nodded shortly to the two brothers. "Thanks."

Like most of the charts that were kept in the Main House, the map Jeffrey had pulled out was labeled with color-coded lines, each of which marked a different route for slave traders based on their customary stops.

Glancing over it, Brent picked out which slavers traveled to port cities, such as Peluma; which ones typically went to towns that bordered the imperial coasts; and which ones went inland in order to transport their slaves to different provinces.

He had Xëri, Aaron and all of his friends to thank for teaching him how to read a map, and even to read in general. After learning how to understand the marks and symbols that were plastered across every chart that he laid eyes on, he came to be intrigued by them, studying them out of sheer interest. Matching the hand-drawn landmarks with their corresponding, real-life forms had become a favorable activity for him and even as he glazed over some of the map's illustrations, he recalled their life-size proportions.

Aaron probably had a full-scale map of half of the Empire in his head thanks to the missions that he'd both stolen away on and been assigned to as a recon scout, he thought. For him, looking at a town's representative dot most likely brought the actual community to his mind in crisp detail.[tv]

"We've received a report from Aizen, one of our intel scouts currently stationed in Gilead." Jeffrey indicated a black dot on the map that marked the village: it was just east of the Adriak Mountains, a spectacular range of alps that ran along Lyrik Province's western border. "Unfortunately, he believes the imperials are getting suspicious of him, so rather than wait and join us for the raid he'll be withdrawing. It's likely he's on his way back already.

"As everyone here knows, the Empire has just celebrated the birthday of its founder, Axelius Arkania," Jeffrey continued. "That said, another holiday caravan is on the move. With its generally shorter route, it won't be traveling for much longer. According to Aizen, it's already gone through the northern parts of Nassaul, northern Lenora, and part of Brusseir.

FAST TRAVEL
CODE: INAPINCH

"You all know that it takes a different route every year. This time, its travels in Lyrik have brought it through Varrone" — he tapped the mark that represented the lakeside town, settled at the base of Lyrik's tallest peak, Mount Julius — "and through these villages." He dragged his finger along an invisible line on the map, which cut through every village along the western edge of the region. "He says it's been sticking to traveling along mountain roads and passes, likely to avoid being attacked."

He pointed to Gilead again. "It should be around here soon. After that it'll enter Heletica's Pass and go through the northern reaches of Odelwhite before breaking cover and heading east, to the fortress city of Bengai." His finger moved to the tiny drawing that depicted the aforementioned locale, situated right on the border of Lyrik and Lenora. "After that, it'll take the royal highway into Cleopa, where it'll be closer to our sister village, Dukaris. It'll be their business from then on."

"Shame the people in Axelius have to miss all the fun," Kro observed, noting how the holiday caravan didn't go anywhere near the provincial capital.

"They'll have their own party, I'm sure," Rufus said.

Kro shrugged. "Still. I wouldn't mind raiding a slave caravan right in those noblemen's faces."

"Hmm…" Ivan stroked his thick, brown beard thoughtfully as he studied the map. "If holiday caravan is staying in mountains, then it will be near Taranis," he realized, "when it goes through Heletica's Pass."

"That's correct." Jeffrey stood upright. "My plan was for us to ambush the caravan while it's in Heletica's Pass. Though, as far as details go on how to map out the attack, we'll have to arrange that here."

"Sounds like a breeze." Brent smiled cheekily. "Haven't been up to Heletica yet. What's the layout like? Aaron?" He looked right at him.

Aaron shifted uncomfortably and glanced around the room. "Uh, actually…haven't been there since…heard there was a landslide…"

Brent frowned skeptically.

Aaron didn't look at him.

"We should have a map of the general region under here. Aaron's right: there was a landslide not too long ago thanks to the summer rains. But, I'm pretty sure we have an updated map…" Ben moved to sift through a pile of documents that were stacked in a slot beneath the table. "One of our recon teams just came back from there and…what the…" He stopped flicking through the maps, almost surprised. "It's not here."

"It might be with some other documents next door," Eve surmised, sighing. "If it was a newer group that did it, they may not have realized that they were supposed to bring it in here. I'll get it." She moved, meaning to exit the room.

As she headed for the door Aaron folded his arms, and then he scratched the back of his head anxiously. "Wait," he said finally, abruptly.

Eve looked at him, as did everyone else.

Rather than look at her, or anyone else in the room for that matter, he kept his eyes glued to an empty spot on the table. "You don't…have to do that."

Eve eyed him suspiciously.

"…I know what the Pass looks like." He raised his head.

Brent smiled daringly. His golden eyes danced. "Well?"

Aaron raked a hand through his messy hair. His next sigh sounded even more defeated than the last. "It's…pretty big," he started carefully and he lowered his eyes once more, picturing the scene in his mind with the utmost detail. "It goes on for about three miles, and it's closed in by two rocky mountainsides. Both are extremely craggy, so there are plenty of footholds and small cliffs that overlook the road."

Brent's eyes twinkled, as if he'd been anticipating Aaron's confession. "The road's straight?"

"No. It switches back in two spots. The landslide was at the second, but all it really did was make the path narrower. Not by much, though. As for everywhere else, the road is straight."

"Sounds like the terrain is tight. The slave traders might be sensitive to that and beef up their security for fear of an ambush." Brent turned his eyes back to the map.

But he wasn't really looking at it. He was trying to envision the place that Aaron had just described.

"How many of those cliffs are there?" he asked. "We'd need a good vantage point."

"I could only make out about eight or nine," Aaron replied, looking up in thought while crossing his arms. "There's a big one right over the first switchback. The second one's got a similar one."

"Are there any good places to climb down from?"

"Some slopes. The cliff over the first has one that's firm enough to walk on."

"And the second?"

"More like a slope, thanks to the landslide."

Brent closed his eyes, his mental image of the mountain pass steadily becoming clearer. "What's your range of abilities would you say?" he inquired next, looking at Tyre and Kro. "With the aether."

"Our influence is as broad as the human imagination!" Tyre said proudly, sweeping his hands across the air.

"Almost." Kro retracted.

"Stick-in-the-mud…" Tyre mumbled. He grunted when Kro punched his arm.

"What about invisibility?" Brent asked.

"We can do that," Kro replied smugly, his arms folded while Tyre rubbed his sore limb.

"On carriages as big as the ones in the holiday caravan?"

"Oh. Um…" Sitting up, Tyre glanced at his elder brother. "One of us'd be able to keep one of those invisible for…I dunno…three minutes?"

"Three minutes on our own, I'd say," Kro agreed and they both refaced Brent. "A lot more people than we're used to will be in the wagons after all."

"Yeah." Tyre nodded his seconding.

A torrent of ideas flooded Brent's brain. "Then —"

"*Wait!*" Ivan burst, his hands up. "Wait, wait, wait, wait, wait. How do you know this? About the Pass?" His eyes were on Aaron, who looked more than uncomfortable now. "As you said: I did not assign you to scout that region since the rainstorm."

"I…" Aaron glanced around then heaved a sigh. "Sometimes,

when my scouting teams go to one place I…" His eyes shifted away. "I go somewhere else. Like Ben said, the last team that went out there wasn't assigned to the Pass, only to that general region. But they were too scared to go in the Pass so, I went alone. I gave 'em my reports after. Would've told them to stick 'em all in here if I'd known they didn't have a clue to."

"Why didn't you say anything when you got back?" Jeffrey questioned.

Aaron closed his eyes and Brent knew he was cursing himself. "I didn't come back with them," he admitted.

Ivan's eyes grew, but his shock was soon darkened by a warning look. "Aaron. We discussed this. You cannot go off on your own."

"Come on, you know how those new guys can be!" Aaron snapped. "Half of 'em are scared that they're gonna get caught and sold back into slavery, so they slack off! 'Sides, it's no big deal. I don't go over the top, I just…" He raised a shoulder half-heartedly and his disgruntled scowl fell to the table. "Fill in the holes."

Ivan's jaw was tight, his eyes hard.

For a moment Aaron refused to look at him. But he could feel his father's gaze burning into him.

At last, he straightened and met Ivan's glare with one that was equally intense.

At length, Ivan sighed. "We will discuss this at later time. For now" — he motioned to Brent — "continue. You speak as if you have plan already. Now: what does the great Skylok have in mind?"

Brent's eyes gained a lively sparkle, and a mischievous smile blazed across his lips.

43

SHORTLY AFTER BRENT'S plan had been approved and the raiders were dismissed, he, Aaron and Liam headed to the foot of the village, just before the farmlands, where they intended to await the rest of their team while they gathered some last-minute supplies. The three young raiders themselves had stopped in the Main House's kitchens after the briefing, which was waking up for breakfast, and there they supplied themselves with rations and canteens of water. Other than that, they were in need of nothing else.

Aaron made himself comfortable on a flat-faced rock while they waited, crossing his heel over his knee, and Brent and Liam stood nearby. The sun was rising and villagers were steadily beginning to awaken; a few roads away, they saw a small group of trainees heading to the sparring hall for an early morning lesson.

"By the way, Liam." Brent faced him after politely greeting an elder, who smiled and nodded as he walked past. "Got any news on what we talked about? With what happened in Lenora."

Liam shook his head.

"What, that stuff about Çaru'qu howling?" Aaron asked. As Brent had promised, he'd shared with Aaron all that the masked stranger had said to him in a bid to have him assist in prying more information out of Ivan. He grunted when Liam confirmed his query. "Yeah. Dad didn't have much to add, either."

"A dead-end, huh?" Liam deduced.

"Looks that way," Brent said, disappointed.

"'Çaru'qu doesn't make mistakes' and something howling…" Aaron sat back on his hands and frowned. "Honestly, the hardest thing to believe about any of this is Brent being a 'chosen one'."

"Heh." Liam turned aside, but Brent had already heard him.

"It's not *that* hard to believe!" he protested.

Aaron didn't turn. "Then why'd you decide to keep that part from Mom and Dad?"

Brent turned away to reflect upon this, and his eyebrows angled together. "…Pops doesn't seem to know all that much about this whole Çaru'qu thing," he said at last. "Even if I did tell 'em, think it'd be best if I had a bit more to go off of first, for my own sake. More than what some guy in a mask can tell me, anyway."

"Huh." Confusion entered Aaron's expression. "Wait a sec. Last year, after you graduated." Sitting up, he twisted to see Brent. "Didn't you say you heard something roaring over the valley? Up by Adelle's grave."

"Yeah, and you said I probably ate something and imagined it."

"That was before some freak showed up saying that it meant something." Aaron scowled at the earth. "Looks like we really might have to find the answers for ourselves after all. For all we know, Dad doesn't know half as much as that guy suggested. Could've been a bad lead from the start."

"Thinkin' to sneak off again?" Brent asked with a crafty smile. "Pops is already on to you, y'know."

Aaron grunted.

"He's right," Liam consented. "I'm almost surprised you blew your own secret."

"Shut up," Aaron huffed, planting his elbow on his leg and dropping his chin into his hand.

Brent grinned. "You know what they say," he said to Liam. "What you've done in the dark will be made known in the light!"

"Who says that?" Aaron frowned at him.

"I'm not sure that's how it goes." Liam looked a tad confused.

Brent would've responded, but a pair of approaching footsteps led him to turn around instead.

He smiled at who was coming near. "Hey, Ren."

"Morning!" the girl returned, and Liam and Aaron shifted to see her as well. "I came to see you guys off."

"Aww, thanks!" Brent grinned.

Renée noticed his reaction. "I'm guessing your briefing went well?"

"That depends on how you look at it," Aaron grumbled.

Renée's confusion wasn't difficult to miss.

"Don't mind him." Brent waved a hand at Aaron. "He's just mad cuz he blew his own cover."

It took Renée a second to understand. "Oh! You mean about his secret recon trips? I'm honestly kind of surprised you still do that." She quirked an eyebrow at Aaron. "I thought you would've stopped after you graduated."

"A rebel's job is never done," Liam said.

"You don't know how right you are," Aaron sighed.

"Yeah, well, today he finally spilled the beans all on his own. Not that it was that much of a secret, really." Brent looked at Aaron. "Toldja it'd come out at some point, *oçachevi.*"

"*Uvuçai!*" Aaron snapped.

Brent's teeth flashed in entertainment.

"Oça…chevi?" Renée repeated.

"Blabbermouth," Liam translated.

Renée blinked, surprised that he knew the answer.

"What?" Brent rounded on him. "I didn't know you knew Aionbo, Liam."

"I'm not fluent," he said.

"Oça…chevi," Renée said again, more so to herself.

Brent laughed. "Trying to get it down, Ren?"

"I was…well…" A light pink entered her cheeks. "I've only ever heard you, Aaron and a few other Avats in the village speak it. It sounds kind of cool."

"Wanna learn? It's easy! Compared to Katruskan anyway." Brent smiled brightly. "The vowels are the easiest to get. They're the same as in Arkanian, but the difference is they've only got one sound each."

"Really?" Renée couldn't deny her curiosity.

"Yeah! They've only got long vowel sounds. In fact, with just them, you could probably carry out a whole conversation."

"Seriously?" She frowned. "How?"

"Like…" Brent tapped his chin and nodded like he was listening to someone explain something profound. "Ahh." He cringed at a follow-up phrase. "Ee…" His eyes became round with interest. "Ooh!" He made a face like he couldn't believe what he'd just heard. "Ehh?" His eyebrows rising, he framed his chin with his thumb and index finger. "Ohh!"

"Oh! So like…" Renée nodded as if someone had successfully explained something to her. "Ahh." She winced at a disappointing remark that followed. "Ee…" Holding her cheeks, her eyes became wide and child-like. "Ooh!" Clapping a hand to her chest, she leaned back in bewilderment. "Ehh?!" Straightening, she popped her fist into her palm. "Oh!"

Brent laughed. "Exactly! You're pretty good!"

"Well, I do have a good teacher," Renée returned, honest and sheepish all at once. When Brent smiled at her, she felt her face get hot.

"Vowels are just the start," Liam interrupted flatly. "Next there are consonants, conjugations, sentence structures, honorifics…"

Renée smiled weakly. "Maybe I should just take it one step at a time for now."

"I thought you said you only knew a little," Brent said to Liam.

"I said I'm not fluent."

"By the way," Renée looked from Liam to Brent, "was the chief upset? About Aaron."

Brent and Liam looked at Aaron, who was clearly trying to ignore them.

"Let's just say he might not be alive for much longer," Liam offered.

Renée was disappointed. "That bad, huh?"

"Can't be helped. Doesn't look good when one of the chief's own sons doesn't listen to him."

"Ah…that's a good point…"

"Yeah. Shame." Brent shot Aaron an impish smile. "We should probably start planning your funeral now, *oçachevi*. Save us the trouble later. I'll give the eulogy in Katruskan as a favor. Or d'you prefer Aionbo?"

"You're not getting anything in my will," Aaron retorted.

"Aw, c'mon, I held up my end of the deal! Not *my* fault you blew it."

"Yeah, to help you make a plan!"

"You're right. Thanks for taking one for the team!"

"I hate you."

"Love you, too, bro."

Turning away from them, Liam's silver eyes fell to Renée. She was watching the pair with a sad sort of smile. "Something wrong?"

"Huh?" Startled, she hurriedly tried to compose herself. "Oh, n-no, not really. It's…" Her brow crinkled sadly. "It's just that…"

Liam watched her with a scrutinizing stare. Before he could question her further, he heard the sound of footsteps approaching.

He turned.

The rest of their raiding team was coming. Led by Ivan, they'd all equipped their weapons to their sides or to the backs of their belts, and hanging over their shoulders were small satchels and waterskins.

"Ah, Renée!" Ivan greeted, spotting her. "You are up early! You have come to see the boys off as well?"

"Yeah." Renée smiled. "Just to offer support. But I'm sure they'll all be fine. They always are."

Ivan nodded his agreement and turned to the three raiders with her. "So, you are ready to go?"

"Ready." Aaron got to his feet.

"We still must talk when you return," Ivan said as his son came closer and stepping forth to meet him, he clapped his large hands onto his shoulders. "But for now, take care of yourself. Watch out for each other. Road to Pass is not easy."

"We'll be fine," Aaron assured. "See you when we get back."

Ivan only nodded silently.

"We should get going," Jeffrey said decidedly, starting towards the valley. "Caravan'll be there tonight. The sooner we get to the Pass, the better."

"Yes. This is true." Looking at Brent, Aaron and Liam, Ivan twice beat his chest and held his fist in place. "Safe travels to you all."

Renée assumed his position. "We'll be waiting for you when you get back."

"Right." Aaron saluted back to them, then tossed his hand up in a wave before descending into the valley along with the others.

Adjusting the satchel of supplies that he'd slung over his shoulder, Brent walked away with him. "Later!"

Liam joined with a quiet nod of farewell to Renée and the chief.

"Try not to miss me," Kro said as he walked past Renée, gently touching the spot beneath her chin, and the friendly smile that she'd been wearing left her.

"Quit it, Kro, you're annoying her!" Tyre pushed his sibling away from her as he moved into the valley, but he made sure to holler a quick, "Later, Ren!" over his shoulder as he did.

"I'll come back for you!" Kro shouted and Tyre hit him over the head, which encouraged the older boy to pull him into a headlock as they continued into the low-lying fields.

Renée's eyes drifted over the brothers and rested on Brent, Aaron and Liam, who were marching along at the group's front.

Her face saddened. "It's…been like this for what feels like forever," she said.

Ivan looked to her.

"Our skill levels were staggered back when we were trainees," she said. Though she addressed the chief, she kept her eyes on the group of raiders as they journeyed into the valley. "Aaron and I were pretty closely matched, and Liam caught up fast when he got here. But Brent…he lagged, for a while. Then, he caught up, too. Looking back, it's like it happened in the blink of an eye. Now, it feels like I'm the one who's always hanging behind." She pushed her lips together, her eyes narrowing in the daylight.

At last, she let out a sigh.

"I have heard only good things from sparring hall about you, Renée." Ivan faced her and she looked up at him. "You are an inspiration to younger raiders. I have even heard some of the little girls want to become raiders because of you. Like Lilian." He chuckled.

Renée glanced away, embarrassed.

"And do not see becoming a raider as a competition." Ivan was grave now. "We are not training raiders for purpose of idolizing them. No…the Liberation Fronts, we serve purpose. We fight to free those who have been told they have no right to life. No hope. No home."

Renée looked into his face again.

"You will not be compared to Brent, Aaron, or Liam, when you join them." Ivan's beard shifted as he smiled and he looked out into the valley. "You will not be compared to Terra, either."

Renée paused, watching him as she allowed his words to sink in. With a calm morning wind touching her cheeks and causing her hair to dance, she looked towards the valley alongside him. This time, rather than looking to the raiders who'd gone ahead of her, she peered towards the horizon. Towards the sunrise.

Towards the Empire.

"But, you must now decide for yourself," Ivan went on and he watched her profile. "Do not compare yourself anymore. *You* have chosen this path, Renée. Why do you choose to keep walking it?"

Renée's eyes fell to the ground silently, and she considered.

He was right. For most of her life she'd done nothing but compare herself: to her mother, to her father, to Aaron, to Liam, to Brent. And now, with her graduation only a short few days away, she was still doing it. It drove her into arguments with her mother, wrestled with her in the sparring hall during every training session. It wore on her.

She took a breath, a deep one, of this sweet morning air, and closed her eyes. For a short moment she let those frustrations bleed out of her, just enough for her to determine if there was something else lying beneath them.

She'd never even allowed herself the time to do this before. But now, just in this moment, if she could just take advantage of this one, small space of time…

For the first time in a long while, a strange peace pervaded her. And she found it —

That something else lying beneath.

"You're right, Chief," she said, her eyes opening.

Her shoulders felt lighter, lifted as she came to the realization that she'd always had the answer. The only problem was that she'd never thought to speak it, not even fully acknowledge it.

But now, she would. "But only half-right."

He cocked his head, interested. "Half-right?"

"At first, I chose this path because everyone around me did." Renée had never truly thought to consider that possibility, although it had crossed her mind a few times over the last several months. Why had she decided to train to become an auction raider? Was it for some altruistic reason, like her father and mother's? Or was it simply out of a desire to follow what had looked like the flow of popular thought at the time?

She hadn't wanted to question it for too long, worried that it would lead her to have second thoughts about her choice of trade. If she decided to abandon it she could always go into weaving, like Eklaire, or jewelry-making, perhaps. Maybe even engineering.

But none of those callings had ever sat right with her. Whenever she'd assisted someone with one of those trades, it had always felt temporary. Training in the sparring hall, learning how to defend herself and others…that had always been what had driven her to get up in the morning.

And maybe, deep down, that was what drove her to war against her mother. Because she couldn't bear the thought of being denied the right to defend the defenseless. Somewhere down the line, at some indeterminate point in time, that truth had sunken into her, motivated her. She hadn't even noticed it.

Until now.

"I may have chosen this path…but this path chose me, too." She looked at Ivan boldly. "So, I'll follow it to the very end. Until every slave can have the right to live. Until all of them can exist in this world without fear."

It was a genuine answer, from her heart. Ivan could see it plainly.

She reflected him, in a way, though they weren't even related by blood. After all, he'd spoken similar words himself, decades ago.

He smiled at her. "I believe you will, Renée."

Determination drew on Renée's brow and when she looked towards the mountains again, it shone in her eyes.

She believed it, too.

44

KEEPING HIS EYES pinned to the entrance of Heletica's Pass, Brent quieted his breathing so much that it nearly blended with the wind.

Around him Liam, Jeffrey, Tyre and Eve were just as tense, none of them daring to even make the smallest of movements. Brent didn't even consider twitching when an itch nagged him from the tip of his nose.

He and the others had arrived at Heletica's Pass only a short few hours after dusk. By now, the last of the sun's rays had long-since disappeared beneath the hilly skyline.

Splitting their groups into two, with Brent, Tyre, Eve, Liam and Jeffrey headed for the first switchback while Aaron and the others went for the second, they waited in stony silence for the holiday caravan to arrive. To anyone passing by below, the slave auction raiders would have looked like nothing more than little rocks, or perhaps ancient carvings from civilizations that predated even the Arkanian Empire.

The pass looked exactly as Aaron had described it. At one end the cobbled, provincial carriageway wound into view and plowed ahead for roughly a mile, then twisted around the switchback that Brent was stationed at and barreled on for another half a mile. After that it wrapped around the second switchback — where Aaron and his team were lying in wait — and went on for another mile and a half before it squeezed through a narrow trail formed by a collapsed ridge.

The landslide.

After that, it stretched into Odelwhite Forest and disappeared.

What Brent found to be the most appealing about the land's geography was that even though the pass followed the descending slope of a mountain, the craggy walls that surged out of the great hill bordered it like the enclosure of a maze. So, even when one part of the holiday caravan was on a trail that was higher than the other, the slave traders still wouldn't be able to see each other.

It was perfect.

He fixed his eyes on the start of the road.

Something was coming.

Hunkering down, he stared unblinkingly at the pass's entrance. Soon, the sound that he'd caught increased until he could define it as the rattle of metal wheels.

He listened harder.

The grunt of an animal jumped at his eardrums.

An auroch.

That was typical. Holiday caravans tended to be larger than regular slave carriages, and so aurochs were the only creatures capable of hauling them around. Born with genes that enabled them to grow to about twice that of a horse, they were large creatures with thick ivory horns that curved around their lips, and big black eyes that were steeped into long faces. Their shoulders hunched like hills due to their musculature, and they boasted enough strength to charge straight through a concrete building if they so desired. Pulling two carriages full of people would be more than an easy charge for them.

It would also distract them.

Stilling himself, Brent picked up the sound of the animals' heavy hooves pounding across the soil, as well as the faint tinkle of their harnesses ringing together. Soon a soft, orange light bled onto the walls of the pass, growing in strength as it steadily got closer.

At long last, the hairy features of two aurochs broke around the bend. They trudged forth on short, bulky legs and soon, a second pair of them emerged from around the corner.

After that, the first half of the holiday caravan appeared in its entirety.

Surrounded by three slave traders on horseback, the first two cars of the caravan bore a slight resemblance to traditional slave carriages: there was a rectangular slot in the front of the first car — which the driver could use to shout at the slaves if the need or urge arose — as well as small, square openings that edged the roofs, allowing air to circulate throughout the vehicles' interior. Two lanterns dangled from curved poles at the front of the first car, and their glass encasements shuddered with every bump in the dirt road.

The carriages themselves were much bigger than average. They were wide and rectangular, and they even had a series of calligraphic markings and colorful images painted on their faces. Their roofs were cusped gables, and above the head of the driver there was a wooden carving of Empyrean, with its wings spread and beak opened wide. Vedrah hissed silently beneath it, and eight shadowy figures leaned against the walls of both carriages. They were supported by a sturdy foot bar as well as a hand bar.

Despite his distance, Brent knew that the dark silhouettes were slave traders. In fact he could hear them, for their chainmail jostled noisily as they traveled along. Every clink of their metallic tunics ricocheted between the high walls of the pass, leaving it to ring in his sensitive ears at a magnified level.

Once they'd made it halfway down the path the clatter of wheels, grunting of aurochs and clanking of armor doubled, drawing his gaze back to the entrance of the pass.

There, the second half of the holiday caravan was coming into view.

"Tyre," Brent called softly. "Check the second group. Who's got the signal horn?"

Having looked at Brent to learn what he wanted to say, Tyre faced away and reached into a small pouch that was tied to his waist. Flipping it open, he reached inside and pulled out a monocular that was little more than four inches long.

Flicking the brass cover off, he raised it to his eye and scanned the slave traders' magnified expressions.

"The horseman on the left has it," he said quietly. "It's on his hip."

"All right. That's your target. We can't let him call for help." Brent lowered his eyes to the first half of the holiday caravan and he waited until it rounded the first switchback below.

Once it had, he motioned to Jeffrey. Then with careful steps, he soundlessly led his group off of the overhang and down to the road.

Following a narrow, descending trail that broke away from their lookout point Brent moved stealthily, his footfalls as soundless as a feline inching towards its prey.

Behind him the others crept forth just as noiselessly, their feet skirting around loose stones and their forms shifting gracefully between the shadows.

Closer to the road, there was a large slab of rock that hid the trail from outside eyes. It was there that Brent stopped, encouraging the others to do the same.

"Okay..." He tilted his eyes to Tyre. "You're up."

Tyre grinned. Rolling his shoulders, he hopped down to the road.

As he did, his approach hidden by the darkness, one of the slave traders that was riding the first carriage yawned loudly.

"Don't sleep on the job, Murdoch," a colleague behind him said.

"I can't help it..." The thick, bald man yawned again, louder than before. "I'm just so tired...and my hand's all cramped around this bar..." He swapped the hand that was holding the iron bar with his free one and stretched his fingers.

"You shouldn't complain," his younger comrade chastised and his voice jumped a bit as they skipped over a bump. "After all, we're trying to get these slaves across the entire Empire before the holiday season's over. If we break too often we'll have to slash the discounts, and that'll make a lot of people angry."

"Yeah, yeah..." Murdoch continued to flex his fingers, his face knit into a deep frown. "I just can't wait 'til we get to that rest stop up ahead. I'm looking forward to another good night's sleep."

"It's not even that late."

Murdoch scoffed. "Let's just say I'm tired of taking these devils and their friends all over the place. They reek. My nostrils sting. I'm too old for this."

The slaver behind him smirked humorously. "And to think, you're the same Murdoch Macrinus who had the chance to work under *the* Captain Alrik. Thought you'd be more excited about something like this."

"That was years ago," Murdoch replied sourly. "After the captain was drafted into Empyrean's Guard, our whole unit was put under a younger recruit who turned out to be an inexperienced nightmare. Moving my whole family to northern Lenora was the smartest thing I'd ever done. Never thought I'd get stationed on the holiday caravan, though. Didn't think I'd step foot back in Lyrik until well after I'd decided to retire in Peluma or something."

"Well…does it feel good to be back in Lyrik early, at least?" his comrade asked, and a teasing lilt entered his voice. "It's the place where you first met your wife, had your first child…"

Murdoch released something like a laugh and a snort while his comrade sniggered. "Quiet, you. You'll be meeting your wife soon enough!"

"Hope so…is Valentina seeing anyone?"

Murdoch suddenly rounded on him with bug-eyed intensity. "Why are you asking about my daughter?"

The younger slave trader balked. "I —"

Before he could answer, a sharp whistle perforated the night.

Murdoch nearly fell off the carriage.

At the same time the horseman to their right started, for the horn that had been hanging from his belt had dropped to the ground as if someone had cut it clean off his waist.

Murdoch and the young slave trader behind him stared questioningly as the horseman slowed his steed to retrieve it.

But right when he moved to slip out of the saddle a current of wind gathered around him, playing with his hair until it grew to a strength that forced him to squint.

In no time at all, the wind surged to a force that was strong enough to make the horn move: mere inches at first, then half a foot. Finally, with the burst of a powerful gale that scared the man's horse, it was vacuumed into the darkness up ahead.

The driver of the wagons started, as did the aurochs, and he looked around to find what had zoomed past him. He soon became aware of a figure that was standing a little ways ahead of his beasts.

Hauling on the reins, he forced them to halt.

When they did, the being that he'd seen leisurely stepped out of the shadows and into the range of the carriage lanterns.

Instantly, the dancing glow of the flames caught the fleering stranger, illuminating his tasseled clothes and sashes, his jewelry and tribal accessories. It even caught the smooth, white face of the trader's horn, which he was tossing up and down inattentively.

Suddenly realizing what was about to happen, Murdoch's black eyes grew to the size of saucers. He reached for his sword.

But right as he grabbed at the hilt, Tyre tossed the signal horn up one last time, higher than before, and with a flash of light and the licking of bright flames, it exploded in midair.

Shards of ivory rained around him and he chuckled at the horrified astonishment on the slave traders' faces. *"Whoops."*

A light breeze slowly encircled his body and in the blink of an eye it swelled to whirlwind force, consuming the road until the air was choked by soil.

Shouts of surprise died in the men's throats, strangled by the flying dirt, and they squeezed their eyes shut.

"An ambush!" one of them finally managed.

"It's those savages!" another one roared. "Don't let them near the carriages!"

With the cover of dirt thickening and the slave traders' panic growing, Brent drew his bladed staffs and charged in with Jeffrey, Liam and Eve at his sides.

As they neared the edge of the cloud Tyre shifted, shooting a blast of wind from his hand to create an opening on the left. With the other, he forged a clearing on the right.

Jeffrey and Eve raced into the right-side opening. With Liam close behind, Brent sprinted through the tunnel on the left.

Almost immediately they came upon a slave trader who was blinking furiously, his sword drawn as he struggled to peer through the swirling cloud.

Closing the gap between them, Brent smacked the man's blade aside with one staff and then swung them both back. Planting his feet he twisted, slicing through the slave trader's chainmail with one sword and dragging the other across his exposed chest next.

His eyes didn't flicker, didn't even blink at the blood that came out.

As his body fell Liam stepped onto Brent's shoulders and vaulted ahead to drop in front of another slave trader. Countering him with one blow and defeating him with another, he and Brent ran deeper into the dust.

In the midst of all this, Tyre hastened to a lip of land that offered a decent vantage point over the commotion. Settling there, he sent gales blasting to and fro across the battlefield, clearing the way for his allies while altogether blinding their foes.[tv]

Murdoch was caught in one of those gusts. Covering his face with both arms he grimaced as dirt, pebbles and soil blasted his front. When everything died down he tried to look around, but his clogged vision made it impossible.

Suddenly another tornado blew into him and the dust settled.

It was only then that he was able to discern the outline of someone running towards him, staff at the ready.

His skin crawled, and he unsheathed his sword so forcibly that his scabbard went flying. Through the quick winks of his eyes, he caught sight of his attacker's spiky blue hair and the hard resolution — even anger — that shone in his golden eyes.

Murdoch's jaw dropped.

All at once, things that he'd once forgotten leaped to the forefront of his mind: a cabin and barn aflame; a woman imprisoned, charged with treason; and a small goblin-boy, fleeing through the woods in a means to escape the slave traders that hunted him.

How long ago had it been? Six years? Seven?

Back when he'd still been under Captain Alrik, that man who's greed had forced Murdoch and his fellow slave traders to race after a seemingly worthless brat in the hopes that it would fetch a fairer price than the slaves that they'd already captured.

He stumbled backward, his eyes bulging as Brent closed in on him. "It's —! Y-you're —!"

Before he could finish, Brent was upon him. Whirling his staff in a wide arch, he smashed it into Murdoch's head.

The man's world went black.

TOO MUCH FUN?
CODE: HELETICA

Spying Tyre's cloud of dust from his location, Aaron twisted around to face Kro. "We're clear."

Turning away from the same sight, Kro stood on the small ledge that he and his team were on. With his eyes on the first two cars of the unsuspecting holiday caravan below he waved his arm to the side, creating a gust of wind that rammed into the carriages like a sandstorm.

As the slavers shouted, bewildered by the cloud's sudden appearance, Aaron slipped his tonfa out of their holsters and twirled them against his forearms.

Then, he and his team leaped off the ledge and into the cloud.

Just before they fell through it Kro opened holes in the top of it, allowing each of them to see which slavers they were dropping in on.

Rolling upon landing, Aaron hooked the handle of one of his tonfa behind the knee of a slaver and swept him off his feet. Spinning his weapon back against his arm, he moved on to another and dispatched him quickly.

Once he'd fallen, Aaron sprinted further into the dust. A blast of wind from Kro put the caravan's second carriage in his sight.

But before Aaron could close in on it, a slave trader practically fell out of the swirling dirt to attack him.

Spinning away from his sword, Aaron flicked the switch on the end of one of his handlebars. Instantly, its hidden blades exploded into view.

Flipping the short sword along his forearm, Aaron weaved around the slave trader's next attack and slammed the sharp head of his tonfa into his waist. Raking his outer scythe across the man's torso, he ripped free of his flesh and punctured him with his sword.

The imperial crumpled in a heap.

Aaron ran for the carriage again, only to duck into a sliding dodge when the body of a different slaver went flying over him.

Jumping over Aaron, Ben closed in on the imperial, who was scrambling for his signal horn. No sooner had he brought it to his lips did Ben kick it out of his hands and with another, he knocked him out.

Spiraling, he caught Aaron's eye and glanced at the carriage. "Go!" he yelled, waving his sword at it. "I'll cover you!"

Nodding his consent, Aaron sheathed his tonfa and ran to the back of the vehicle, where he skipped onto the lip of wood that jutted out of its back door. In the same instant, he climbed onto the roof.

Breaking into a sprint, he ran for the lead carriage. There, he jumped down to land beside the driver.

The man shouted in surprise and reached for his knife.

Aaron disarmed him with a perfectly straight kick that knocked him clean out of the seat.

No sooner was he airborne did Aaron drop into his chair and seize the reins, pulling on them hard enough to urge the aurochs to do a complete about-face.

Snorting heavily they did so, and the holiday carriages bobbed with the sharp U-turn.

As Aaron drove the caravan back through the pass, the last of the slavers fell at the hands of his allies. Noting the passing carriages, they jumped onto its sides to ride it out of the battlefield.

"We're down on time!" Swinging around, Brent slammed his staff into the face of an advancing slave trader. Pivoting back, he split his weapon into swords and blocked a surprise attack. "Get the carriages!" He cut his ambusher down.

"Already on it!" Dodging around the fallen bodies of slave traders and panic-stricken horses, Jeffrey swung into the front of the caravan, aiming a flying kick in the process and knocking the driver there out of his way. Sliding into his place, he gripped the reins and forced the aurochs to slow.

Growling and snorting, they followed the tug of the reins and turned around, hauling the large carriages back through the pass.

As they marched along, the rest of the raiders hopped onto the cars' sides and grabbed the hand bars to hold steady.

Brent jumped aboard last, leaping onto the lip of wood that stuck out of the last car's back door. From there, he swung onto the roof and crouched when the carriage bounced. When he was steady, his eyes fell to the defeated slave traders.

Tyre jumped off of the ledge that he'd been standing on and landed atop the carriage behind him. There, he dropped to his knees and pressed his hands against its shingled surface.

He exhaled softly, slowly. Then, drawing on the quintessence that dwelled in the depths of his being, he joined the aether.

Almost immediately, Brent shivered.

Twisting around he looked at Tyre, whose hands were glued to the roof of the carriage as a look of strained concentration pulled at his face. His arms were shaking and a strange light of gentle greens and blues was pulsing around them.

But what mesmerized Brent more was the fact that Tyre was completely see-through.

Shuddering again Brent looked at his own hands, his arms, the carriage.

All of it was transparent.

He let out a sigh of awe and all at once, he came to realize that something he couldn't see was pooling over him. It was a heavy, shapeless mass that draped over his body like a weighted blanket — powerful and dominating, warm and yet altogether alien.

The aether.

He cast Tyre a fleeting look before turning back to the road, his sharp ears tuning in to movement.

One of the slave traders was stirring. But given his sluggard movements, it was apparent that he'd only be conscious for a few short seconds.

Still, Brent watched him.

Groaning, Murdoch peered through his foggy vision to see the holiday caravan. Although his vision was shaky, he could tell that it was getting farther and farther away.

Gritting his teeth against a violent throb of his skull, his eyes adjusted enough for him to see that the blue-haired Avat that had bludgeoned him was crouching atop the last car.

The slave traders in Lyrik called him Skylok, if he wasn't mistaken.

No, not just Skylok, Murdoch thought, correcting himself. He would've recognized that blue hair anywhere.

After all, he'd only ever come across it once before.

Just before his world tunneled into nothingness, he saw the boy pull down the skin beneath one of his eyes and stick his tongue out tauntingly.

Then, he and the caravan vanished.

45

AWN HAD CRACKED the sky by the time Brent and the others had arrived at the northeastern barrier that hid the valley of Taranis from the imperial fields. Standing before them as a soaring wall of tangled boughs, massive vines and rebellious boulders, it looked like the result of a horrible landslide that had crashed through a dense forest. There was no way through it and with steep mountain walls crushing it in, there was no way around it, either.

Tyre and Kro leaped off the caravan and approached this blockade without regard for its impression.

"Home stretch." Kro spread his feet and lifted his hands in front of him, left hand ahead of the right. "Still got some juice left in you, bro?"

"Don't worry about me." Tyre took a similar stance, but with his right ahead of his left. Though he was fixated on the barrier, he mimicked his sibling's cocky smile. "I've got some to spare."

"Heh. Just try and keep up."

They inhaled together and exhaled as one, and the hair on their skin rose as they hunted for their inner reserves of quintessence. Grasping it, they released it, causing the lanterns that hung off of the carriages' horns to bobble eerily.

When the gusts finally stilled, the two stretched their hands to the barrier.

Within seconds the tree limbs and branches began to curl aside, and the boulders nestled near them rolled out of the way, leaving the earth to rumble as if claps of thunder were trapped inside of it. It wasn't long before the rest of the way to the valley was revealed, with Taranis' farmlands and the valley's winding river almost directly in front of them.

"Good work," Jeffrey said and he slapped the reins against the aurochs' sides, urging them into the waiting pastures.

When everyone else had crossed into the plains after him, Tyre and Kro sealed the barrier once again.

By the time the group had drawn near to the village's crop fields the moon was fading in the pinkish sky and the sun was crawling over the hilltops, striking the vale with all the glory of morning daylight. Harmless critters flitted about, some poking their tiny heads through tree branches and shrubs to watch the passing party, while others kept themselves well out of sight.

Brent yawned loudly as the carriage he was riding on rolled ever closer to the village. With his hands laced behind his head and one leg crossed over the other, he looked into the lightening sky with tired, teary eyes.

Liam, who was sitting on the opposite side of the gabled roof, simply looked at the road ahead. He seemed distracted.

"Man…" Brent rubbed his face. "These all-nighters never get any easier…" He peeked up at his yellow-haired friend. "What about you? How do you manage this kinda stuff *and* raise Lilian at the same time?"

Liam didn't answer.

Brent shifted to see him better. Being flat on his back, he had to tilt the crown of his head into the roof and stick his chin into the air to get a good look at him. "Liam?"

Liam glanced at him and away. "Sorry. It's just…" He paused.

Brent waited, one eyebrow furrowing.

"…They're quiet." Liam looked ahead. "The slaves. They weren't like that at the barrier."

"Yeah," Brent said, sitting up. "I noticed. But, they're probably just scared. They never know what's going on when we rescue them en route like that."

"I know that." Liam's silver eyes fell to the carriage roof. "But this seems different."

Brent cast him a fleeting but thoughtful look before he dropped his eyes to the carriage. Closing his eyes, he shut away the sounds of the clattering wheels, the snorting of the aurochs, even the chirping of the morning birds. Centering all of his attention on the cart beneath him, he listened.

He couldn't hear anything.

He opened his eyes.

He wasn't entirely sure if that was something to be worried about. He hadn't heard the slaves talking to each other much either but, as he'd explained to Liam, that was normal. They were probably just nervous.

But Liam was one of his teammates, he reminded himself, and for good reason: Aaron excelled when it came to vision and memory but for Liam, it was his ears and perception. If he sensed that something was amiss, then there was no reason for Brent to overlook it.

After all, neither Liam nor Aaron had yet to mislead him.

The carriage came to an abrupt stop just outside of the farmlands, breaking his train of thought.

He and Liam looked up.

"All right." Jeffrey left the driver's bench and hopped to the road. "Let's open these up and let these people out."

Sharing a look, Brent and Liam grabbed their weapons and jumped to the ground.

"What do we do about the aurochs?" Tyre asked as Jeffrey came around from the front of the wagon.

"We'll make them useful." Jeffrey started towards a door that nearly blended into the painted wall of the first car. "We can use them for food, clothes and blankets, which we'll need plenty of if there's as many people here as we thought." He jumped onto the foot bar that was on the side of the wagon and hooked his fingers into an obscure space that appeared to be a handle.

He stopped.

"Something wrong?" Eve asked finally.

Jeffrey didn't answer. He just pressed his ear against the door.

Brent and Liam heard him swear under his breath.

"Get back." His voice was grave.

Without a word, Eve and the others retreated a few steps.

Behind them, Aaron glanced away from the carriage that he'd ridden in on. Its door was already open, and he and the others had begun to let the slaves out. But the tension that he was sensing from the other half of his team made him uneasy.

Jeffrey faced the carriage's door again. Seizing the handle, he pulled it open and hopped to the ground.

Tyre was the first to step away, his eyes widening.

Eve flinched backward with him.

Liam stared.

Brent's heart dropped to his feet.

The slaves were lying on the floor of the wagon bed, chained to it by thick, iron cuffs. There were male and female Avats inside, even children. One closest to the door looked to be an Arkanian girl, whose pale skin was almost translucent compared to the darker tones of her fellow captives.

"By the gods…" Eve breathed.

Brent opened his mouth. Nothing came out.

The slaves were dead.

🙥 ✣ 🙧

Despite how tired he'd been when they'd gotten back to Taranis, Brent found that he couldn't find the wherewithal to sleep after what he'd witnessed.

There was a graveyard in the southernmost reaches of the plain, not far from Heletia Cavern. Jeffrey and Rufus offered to bring the bodies of the slaves there, where they would bury them with the help of the gravediggers.

Fifty-two. That was how many slaves had been in the carriage. That was how many of them had died. Fortunately, the slaves that had been with Aaron and his half of the team hadn't suffered the same fate.

Jeffrey had said that it was something that happened sometimes. The imperials, upon realizing that they were about to lose what they deemed to be precious cargo, would throw a poisonous pouch of smoking herbs into the slave cart during all of the chaos, hoping to kill the slaves before they could be taken away.

No, not killed.

Murdered.

Because in the Empire's eyes, a dead slave was better than a free one.

Brent had learned about such tactics while he'd been in training. And, during the latter years of his days as a trainee, Jeffrey had begun to reveal more morbid details about the fight that he was about to graduate into. But, in all his time as an official auction raider, he'd yet to deal with such gruesome methods on any of his assignments. So far, he'd seen one success after another, and smiles of gratitude on countless Avat faces, even on the faces of the "sympathizers" and supporters who'd gotten themselves enslaved alongside them.

But now...

His golden eyes tightened and he looked out over the valley lake, where he'd retreated shortly after arriving home.

Children were playing in the water, ignorant of what had just happened, and on the shore their chaperoning parents watched over them. Splashing each other and laughing, the kids swam in circles and shouted until they could hear themselves echo between the pines. They even turned it into a contest.

Brent couldn't help but smile at the sight of them. But with the shadow of the slaves' death rising over him again, he looked away with a quiet sigh.

A split second later he lifted his head once more, for someone was circling the lake towards him.

It was Harver.

"Knew it was you!" she grinned as she came closer. "Only one guy in the whole village has got hair like yours!"

"Hey, Harv," he greeted and she sat down on the rocky shoreline next to him. Pushing forward she dropped her feet into the water, just as he had.

They were quiet for a moment, both of them watching the children play while the adults talked along the shore. Some were in the water with their little offspring.

"Been here long?" she asked.

"Not really."

They were quiet again.

"I heard," Harver said finally, looking at him. "About the slaves. One of the moms just came back from the village with food for the kids. She heard Eve and Rufus talking."

Brent didn't reply, but the downward angle of his gaze spoke of his remorse.

"I'm sorry." Harver put her hands in her lap and kicked her feet. "Arkania…right when you think they can't sink any lower, they pull a stunt like that one."

"Jeffrey warned us about it," Brent said at length.

Harver looked up.

Brent leaned forward and clasped his hands over his knees. "While we were training. He warned us that there'd be times where the Empire'd prove that they'd rather kill an Avat before they let him go free. But I…" He recalled the bodies, the pouch of poison that Tyre had quickly been charged to get rid of aetherially —

A riot in the city, a captain who'd actually considered mercy —

He sighed. "I still wasn't prepared. And I feel like we're partly to blame. If we'd been more vigilant…maybe we could've saved them. But instead, they died only seconds away from Taranis. From freedom." His eyebrows drew together, his jaw clenched, and he dug his nails into his skin.

All the frustration, all the anger he felt towards his own short-sightedness and the unfair ending of the slaves he'd only just rescued accumulated into a single obscenity that left him at a dull mutter.

Harver turned her eyes to the lake sadly.

A thought occurred to Brent after a moment. "How come you're down here, anyway? Aren't you usually in your workshop?"

"What, an engineer can't help chaperone some kids?" Harver quipped. "I'm on a break!"

Sitting up, Brent raised an eyebrow at her. "You? You take breaks?"

"I do!"

Brent tilted his head knowingly.

She relented, convicted. "…Sometimes."

Brent laughed.

"Lady Xëri talked me into it," Harver admitted. "I've been working really hard on my project lately…it feels like I haven't seen the light of day in ages! I almost forgot how nice the water is at this time of year."

"Project?" Brent repeated. "You mean the one that you won't tell anyone about?"

"That's the one!" Harver winked.

"Wait." He squinted at her. "Is this the same project that people have been reporting to Pops about? With these weird sounds coming from your workshop at night?"

"I don't know what you're talking about." Harver turned away smartly.

"You have to let us know what it is at some point. You keep raving about it."

"You'll find out when everyone else does, Mr. Popular!" Harver said, poking his forehead. "I don't share my secrets. Not even with the chief's kid."

"Not even if that chief's kid was Aaron?" he asked mischievously.

If Harver's dark skin could turn scarlet, it did. "Shut up! I-I mean no!"

He laughed. "Maybe I should just send him your way and have him tease it out of you!"

"Tease?! What're you thinking to have him do?!"

"I'll leave that to your imagination, Harv."

"Shut up…!"

He laughed again.

Harver blew her lips and turned from him, only to do a double-take when someone suddenly burst through the trees leading back to Taranis and stumbled into the open.

Her face lit up. "Eklaire!" Lifting an arm, she waved at her. "Hi!"

Eklaire looked around and upon noticing Harver and Brent, she sprinted towards them, relieved. The closer she came to them, the more they noticed that her cheeks were flushed and she appeared to be out of breath. It looked as if she'd sprinted all the way from her home at the bottom of the main road.

Harver's eyebrows puckered.

Brent stood up, some part of him wondering if there was trouble related to the dead slaves from earlier. "What happened?" he asked as soon as she was within reach, and she doubled over to grip her knees.

Worried, Harver got to her feet and came nearer. "Eklaire? Is everything okay?"

The white-haired girl sucked in one last breath before attempting to reply. "Brent, y…y-ya'll…ya'll have to…y…" She stopped again, completely winded. "Whew! Sorry, just…hah!"

"Calm down, Eklaire," Brent told her, although he was growing rather restless thanks to her original urgency. "Try to catch your breath first."

"B-but…but you…need to come quick!" Straightening up, she pumped her fists out in front of her chest. "It's…it's Ren and Terra! They're 'bout to have a brawl over at the sparrin' hall!"

46

S PRINTING FROM THE lake and back to the village, Brent, Harver and Eklaire rushed for the sparring hall. Upon breaking between the houses that lined Taranis' southern side, they hastened past the schoolhouse and closed in on the crowd that was clogging the sparring hall's doors.

Without stopping Brent slipped into the assembly, shouldering his way through to get inside.

Harver did the same and a few feet behind her so did Eklaire, her face pinched with worry.

After much bumping and weaving they finally reached the hall's interior. There, they saw two figures standing in the room's center.

Terra was on the right, her long dagger in one hand and her left arm encased in a silver gauntlet. The fingers extended into sharp, dagger-like claws, likely for slashing at her opponents when they were within range.

Still just as lean and limber as she'd been since her early days as a warrior, the woman commanded a certain attention that rendered all who looked upon her to regard her with awe. Her hair, sheared into a boyish undercut with long bangs, glistened with a certain luster in the light that fell through the hall's windows. Her eyes were just as bright.

At present she was glaring at Renée, who was standing opposite her.

She, too, was armed, her straight sword hanging at her side.

Like her mother, her eyes burned fiercely.

But somewhere beneath the glow, there hung a hesitance that bordered on dread.

Brent's eyes jumped between them before dropping to a boy who was standing nearby. Recognizing him, he put a hand on his shoulder. "Mekial."

Starting, Mekial whirled to find who was speaking to him. "Brent!" he exclaimed and his once anxious frown dissolved. "And Harver! And Eklaire, too!"

As he called out their names the heads of two others that were next to him turned around: Aaron and Liam.

"What's going on?" Brent asked, looking between them.

"Everyone's saying it's just a sparring match," Liam answered. "But, I think it's more than that."

"It's a challenge," someone near Aaron piped up, having overheard Liam's words.

At the sound of her voice, the group turned to her.

She was Elma, the mother of Lacey, a little girl who, like many of the children in the village, had taken a strong liking to Brent and his friends. With her half-lidded eyes and round face, she looked like an older version of her child.

"What do you mean?" Aaron regarded her with a perplexed look on his face.

"Terra challenged Renée," Elma elaborated. "I think it has to do with Terra thinking she's not cut out for raiding. I can't blame her though…it's scary, what's happening to all of the other villages. She's probably thinking that if she lets Renée complete her training and become a raider, something terrible'll happen and she might never see her again…"

"Seriously?" Aaron raised his eyebrows and refaced the fighters.

"It's true," Mekial confirmed. "Dad was trying to get Mom to supervise the last few days of Ren's training or something, cuz they've been arguing about Ren's training a lot more lately. But she didn't want to. Then outta nowhere she decided that if Ren could beat her in a fight she'd let her graduate!"

"Oh, I hope it don't get ugly…" Eklaire prayed behind him.

Brent stared at Terra, baffled by her actions. She was that desperate to keep Renée from becoming a raider?

"Are you ready?" Terra widened her stance and her voice sounded clearly enough for Renée to hear it above the villagers' chatter.

"Mom…" she began, but she suddenly opted to hold her tongue and look away, her eyebrows furrowing with troubled reluctance.

"We talked about this already." If Terra felt any kind of sympathy, it was well masked beneath her harsh features. "Back out now, and you're not training under Jeffrey anymore."

Renée frowned indignantly. "I wasn't —"

"You've been studying since you were a child, haven't you?" Terra broke in. "Own that. Show me that I didn't make a mistake in allowing you to keep at it for this long. Show me you've got what it takes to survive."

Renée didn't respond, but the emotional turmoil within her was clearly visible on her face.

Her expression only faded a little when a familiar voice broke into their ears, booming, *"Wait!"*

Everywhere heads turned, and soon those who were further outside began to jostle and shift, shuffling around in order to make way for the man that was approaching. In time the wave of movement rippled to the front, enticing Brent and his friends to part as well.

By then Ivan's great form was perceived, squeezing through the growing gap in the crowd until he was inside of the hall. With his dark, bushy eyebrows deeply knit, he marched to a spot that was only a few feet away from Terra and Renée.

"Terra," he called as he slowed to a halt and behind him, the throng of people shushed one another. "Is this *really* necessary?"

Terra scowled at him and when she answered, her gaze switched back to Renée. "It is." Though she caught the deepening of Renée's anxious frown, she continued. "Maybe you still believe that our children can take up arms and fight against a tyrannical empire, Ivan. But I *don't.*" Her eyes seemed to shoot icicles with that final word. "I should've gone with my gut from the very beginning. They should stay here, where it's safe."

"Then why must you *fight* your own *daughter?*"

"…To find out if it's possible for me to see what you see," she replied lowly. "I'm giving her the chance to prove me wrong. And if she can't —" her dark eyes swiveled back to him — "she's not going out there. And neither is my son."

At this exchange of dialogue some of the people in the crowd sucked in a breath and began to mutter amongst one another in surprise.

"I thought it was just a sparring match!" Aaron heard someone exclaim.

"That's Terra for you," Harver murmured dully and beside her, Brent's eyes darted from one side of the crowd to the other until he found who he was looking for.

"Ben!" He called out to the man who was standing a few people away from him on his left. "You're fine with this?"

Ben tilted his gaze to see Brent, then returned it to Renée and Terra. "If there's one thing I know about Terra, it's that she's someone who needs tangible proof of something. But I have complete faith in Ren. She'll get through this. No need to worry." He looked at Brent out of the side of his eye with a half-hearted smile.

"It's okay, Chief." Renée's voice drew Brent's attention next, as well as Ivan's. Her eyes were on her mother. "I have to do this."

Terra set her jaw and her eyes narrowed dangerously.

"She wants to gauge me for herself." Lifting a hand, Renée untied the feathered accessory that was wound into her hair and wrapped the rest of her locks into a bun. As she worked, her long, split bangs collapsed around her face. "This is the only way that she'll believe in me."

To hold the loose bun in place she tied her decorative hairpiece around it, leaving its feathers and beads to dangle above her nape. With her hair now out of the way, she unsheathed her sword. "Besides…even Jeffrey thinks that I'm just as good of a fighter as Brent, Aaron and Liam." She shot him a little smile. "So I have to do this. I have to make her see that I'm not just some…helpless little girl. That I fight…for the sake of every slave I'll come across. To defend the defenseless. Not to follow everyone else." She turned a frown of resolution onto her mother. "That I fight for me."

Ivan didn't respond, the disapproving look still carved into his face. But, accepting that the final decision was up to her, he relented with a curt nod.

"You can do it, Ren!" Mekial cheered, cupping his hands around his mouth. "Or, well…you better do it, Ren! My raiding career's riding on this, too!"

"No holding back," Terra stated. "That goes for me as well."

Renée nodded and out of the side of her eye, she saw Ivan move to grant them more room. As soon as he did, a flash of blue entered her vision.

Without particularly meaning to, she honed in on Brent's face. Surprise darted across hers.

He, however, didn't appear to be stunned by her seeing him. Instead, with his eyes holding hers, he dipped his chin silently.

He didn't have to like what was happening. But at the very least, she had his support.

Pursing her lips, Renée bobbed her head in answer. Then, she refaced her mother and spread her feet in preparation.

With her grim features unchanging, Terra raised her long dagger with a backhanded grip and held her gauntleted arm above it.

Seeing this the entire crowd tumbled into silence, watching with bated breath to see how the battle would begin.

Renée spun her sword and then, tilting the blade along the angle of her arm, she raised her opposite elbow and stretched her fingers.

Thus poised in their selected stances she and her mother locked themselves in a soundless standoff, waiting to see who would make the first move.

With their breath nearly absent the crowd watched, their bodies tense. Here and there, eyes flitted between Renée and Terra in restless anticipation.

Finally, Terra leaned on the toes of her rear foot and launched into a breathtaking sprint. With her knife dancing into a new grip, she swiped at her daughter.

Whipping her sword out, Renée knocked Terra's weapon offcourse and wheeled inside of her guard, her pommel coming up to crash into her cheek.

Terra whirled out of range, the wind nearly snapping when Renée hit nothing, and she lunged again, feinting for Renée's throat so as to end the fight.

But Renée stuck her sword in front of her face, blocking the strike, and she twisted on the spot, her sunlit blade circling in a downward arc.

Terra deflected the blow when it came, shattering the air with a thunderous peal of metal, and again she flipped her knife around. Her black eyes blazed and with all the aggression of a ravenous beast, she seized the offensive.

Almost immediately Renée was forced to retreat, parrying her mother's rapid, circular strikes with a defense that was just as swift. The air was filled with the din of ringing metal.

Resurrected from their silence the crowd surrounded the pair with cheers and whoops as they sliced, swiped and dodged around one another. But in spite of their positive energy, Brent felt himself internally wince at every close call that Renée had.

Terra was a close-range fighter with a preference for submissive holds and throws, not to mention violent swipes of her gauntleted, clawed hand. Even though they were related, he was certain that Terra would use any attack at her disposal if Renée left even the smallest of openings.

Renée was aware of this as well, and he knew it. He could see it in her pointed gaze as she watched Terra's movements, identifying when to take the offensive and when to fall back.

Standing on the sidelines, he could only hope and trust that she'd be victorious. After all, if she really meant to prove herself to Terra, she had to remember that this match would ultimately determine whether or not her years as a trainee had been fruitful.

But even with that kind of pressure riding on her shoulders, Brent couldn't doubt her. And it wasn't because he didn't want to — it was because he just couldn't.

Although it was true that Renée was kind-hearted and gentle, he knew that in spite of such traits she was more than capable of handling herself in a fight. There wasn't any reason for him to worry at all.

So even if he didn't agree with it, if this was the only way for Terra to learn of Renée's strength, then so be it.

"U-urgh…d-d'you see 'em yet?"

"No…lift me higher!"

One of the Arkanian village children, Kurt, who was on his hands and knees just outside of the sparring hall, scrunched his face and pushed himself up as high as he could possibly go. Coils of his wild, blonde mane hung about his twisted expression and shone like golden thread in the light of the sun. His arms, scrawny since they belonged to a thirteen-year-old boy, trembled.

Dillon, a boy of fourteen years at present, craned his neck as he stood on his back, and he fastened his green eyes onto one of the sparring hall's high windows. Although it was far above his head, his half-Avat ears could still pick out the clang of weapons ringing behind it, along with the cheers of the crowd.

He reached up to the window, his teeth clenching with effort. But when his fingertips couldn't even graze the sill, he slumped back down with a huff.

He and his friends hadn't been able to push through the crowd to see the fight between Renée and Terra. So he'd led them here, to one of the outer walls, thinking that if Kurt gave him a boost he'd be able to peek through a window and relay what was happening to the others.

But it didn't seem like that was going to work.

Mekial was lucky he was Renée's brother. He probably had a front row seat.

The side of his mouth went up in thought. Then, he laid eyes on the tall, flat boulder that sat beside him.

His face lit up and while standing on top of Kurt, he turned to the boulder and started to climb onto it instead.

"Be careful, Dillon!" Lacey called up to him anxiously, realizing what he was doing. An Avat girl of twelve years old now her long, black hair was tied loosely at the bottom with a violet ribbon, and her small, brown face was drawn with concern.

"Hurry *up*, Dill…" Kurt grunted beneath him. "My arms are shaking…!"

"I still think Kurt should've climbed on *your* back," Klarys said, her beaded arms folded across her chest. Her brown skin was pinched into a disapproving scowl just above her dark eyes. Similar to Dillon, she was one of the oldest of their group.

"He wouldn't have been able to reach the window!" Dillon told her, struggling to haul himself atop the large rock. He pumped one of his feet for leverage.

"*You* can't reach the window!"

Dillon ignored her and when the last of his weight left Kurt's back, the boy fell over with a heavy groan.

"My back's never gonna be the same again!" he cried.

"Are you okay, Kurt?!" Lacey dropped next to him.

"I'll be okay…I think…"

"Whudduyu see, Dill?" Lilian shouted up at him just as the crowd released a synchronized cry of shock. Though only seven, she'd gotten into the habit of hanging out with the older boys and girls, who never seemed too bothered by her company.

"U-um…" Balancing on his knees, Dillon steadied himself on top of the boulder and leaned against the hall to peek through the window. "I-I think Renée just went on the offensive!" His voice shook as he nearly fell.

"Be *careful*, Dill!" Lacey warned again as she and Kurt stood up.

"What's happening?" Kurt asked.

"U-uh — well they're still going" — he nearly slipped again — "but it looks like Terra might be winning now…!"

"Oh no!" Lacey exclaimed, her hands over her mouth.

"Come on, Ren!" Lilian hollered at the building. "Show her you can do it!"

Unaware of her encouragement, Renée kept parrying or dodging Terra's attacks. But as her mother continued to hack away at her her focus faltered, and for the smallest of seconds she imagined failure.

At the same time, Terra reverted to lightning-fast strikes that Renée could barely keep up with. Ducking beneath a swipe of Terra's clawed arm caused her to nearly lose her balance, and she was almost tripped by a follow-up kick.

Scrambling to stay upright, she clumsily deflected a one-two strike of her mother's claws and knife.

"Come on, Renée!" Terra growled, her rapid offense disrupting the girl's chance to recover. "Show me what you've got! You can't let your enemy overpower you!"

Smacking the girl's blade aside with her gauntleted arm, she thrust with her dagger.

Instinctively Renée coiled beneath it, drawing her sword into herself, and as she sprang back up her blade shot for Terra's chin.

Retracting her knife Terra arched backward, her teeth clenched as she pulled her face away from the point of her daughter's sword. Dodging it cleanly, she backflipped out of reach.

Upon flipping upright, her eyes met Renée's.

There was no more hesitation there — only fortitude.

She laughed and with a flip of her blade, she took on the same stance that she'd had when the match had started. Despite her smile, there was danger in her eyes. "That's more like it!"

"Yes!" Dillon cheered from his perch.

"What? What happened?" Lacey bounced on her feet.

"Ren's not letting her win easily — whoa." He glanced down to adjust himself. "Ha! This is so cool…! Go, Ren!"

Her resolute expression steadfast, Renée cut her sword at the empty air and rushed her mother, snatching the upper-hand and leaving her to do little more than block the attacks with her gauntlet.

A few times, Terra attempted to switch the roles of the fight.

But Renée always spiraled out of reach with either a swift twirl or coil of her sword, drawing her evasive tactics from the lessons that Jeffrey had given her.

So Terra pushed harder, driving herself forward until at last, she regained the advantage.

Overwhelmed by her mother's adjustment, Renée began to back down. Soon, the concern that she felt within spilled onto her face, and her mind raced with the returning onslaught of the idea that she wouldn't succeed.

Seeing her panic, Brent raised his voice to call out to her: "Renée! *Focus!*"

Renée barred her sword against Terra's dagger. Even though the crowd roared in her ears, Brent's voice made it to her.

Her eyes flitted in his direction. Then, with a grunt, she shoved

Terra away.

He was right.

She needed to focus.

Bending at the knee, she renewed her stance.

Breathe…!

Flipping her knife around, Terra closed the distance between them again. Nearing Renée she pivoted into her, raised her foot —

The shortest blast of wind howled out of her, tearing through her hair and the net of her jacket.

Renée shivered, sensing the gust more than she felt it —

And Terra kicked, striking out with such force that the air snapped, *trembled,* as if something was ripping through it —

Renée dove to her right.

The force behind Terra's kick roared past her and struck the wall. It shuddered —

— and the windows exploded.

A collective gasp ran through the crowd.

Somewhere in their midst, Jeffrey sighed and rubbed his face.

Ben noticed, and he snickered. "Sorry, man."

In the next instant the crowd's excitement returned, manifesting as cheers and waving fists.

Renée glanced at the broken glass before she looked at her mother, wide-eyed.

"What in the high Peaks of Dover was that?!" Eklaire cried.

"Terra the Terrible," Aaron answered, folding his arms with a rather serious look. "Least, that's what some of the raiders call her. There's a reason she's always on the frontlines during her missions."

"Didn't think she'd try to use that move on Ren, though," Liam admitted.

Brent frowned silently.

"She kicked the *air* and broke the *windows!*" Harver exclaimed. "What's up with that?!"

"Whoa!" Mekial's eyes, shining in the daylight, were as wide as saucers. He grinned. "Go Mom —!" He caught himself. "I-I mean, c'mon, sis! You got this!"

Biting down her surprise, Renée jumped to her feet and settled into a new battle stance.

THORNY ROSE
CODE: ULTIMATUM

Spinning her knife, Terra closed in. *tv*

As soon as she was within range, she twisted nearer to Renée and threw another heavy kick her way.

With a dancing sword, Renée pirouetted out of reach.

So Terra kicked again, and again, and again, each move flowing right into the next. Every blow was meant to land, and every blow carried with it the same pressure that had rocked the building earlier. The only reason she didn't break any more windows was due to the angling of her assault.

Renée didn't understand the workings behind the woman's strength. But, she at least knew the danger.

So she kept moving, relying on her speed and nimble steps to keep herself from harm.

It wasn't long before Terra read the girl's moves. Feinting once, she leaped at her with a downward kick.

Renée adjusted quickly, side-stepped the attack, and Terra stomped on the earthen ground instead. It ruptured as if a groundhog was speeding through it.

Renée staggered.

Thinking she'd found an opening, Terra swiped at her with her blade.

Renée ducked and on springing back up, she smacked her blade into Terra's knife, catching it at an angle and sending it spiraling away.

Before Terra could react, Renée spun in a tight circle and swung her foot in a mighty kick that slammed into Terra's cheek.

Fully caught by the blow Terra's whole body went limp, the flesh of her face rolling from the impact. Like a felled tree, she skidded into the ground with a puff of dust.

The crowd drew breath as one, stunned by the match's abrupt closure. Everywhere scattered voices mumbled their surprise to one another, while others questioned after Terra's wellbeing. Still more villagers looked between one another, exchanging impressed looks.

Finally, they cheered as one.

"Whoa-ho." Aaron lifted his eyebrows. "Didn't see *that* coming."

Brent said nothing. Stunned disbelief was plastered all over his face.

"All right!" Dillon shouted, thrusting his fists into the air.

"What happened?" Klarys burst. "Did Ren win?!"

"She — wh-whoa…*whoa!*" Thrown off by his own excitement, Dillon teetered and toppled right off the boulder.

"Dillon!" his friends cried and they lunged to break his fall, which they did when he landed on top of them.

"Mom!" Renée shouted over the crowds and, dropping her sword, she started for Terra's side.

With her face smothered in the crook of her elbow, Terra threw up a hand.

Renée stopped short. "M-Mom, I…I'm so sorry!" She held her hands over her mouth frightfully and continued to babble as the woman got to her feet, one hand cupping her bruised cheek. "I didn't mean — I mean — I didn't wanna — I didn't think! I-it was instinct, I mean, I-I-I'm sorry —!"

"*Quiet,* Ren!" Wiping her face with the back of her hand, Terra pinned her with a stinging glare. "Never apologize to your opponent!"

Renée clamped her mouth shut.

Terra spat on the ground and went to retrieve her fallen weapon. Spinning it, she thrust it into the holster on her hip.

For a moment she stood there, her narrowed eyes fixed on the ground as she contemplated the results of the battle. At last, she lifted her head. Though her scowl was gone, a stern air still hung about her. "Remember that when you face off against the imperials."

Renée stared at her, not sure whether to feel surprised or relieved.

Suddenly, Terra gripped her head with a small moan.

Renée started.

Breaking free of the restless crowd Ben rushed to Terra's side. After murmuring a few words into her ear — to which she responded with a dull nod — he proceeded to guide her out of the hall.

"She'll be all right," he reassured a few of the villagers who were looking on at her concernedly, and he gently brushed them aside to make a path. As he neared Brent and his friends they, too, shuffled out of his way.

Only Brent's eyes moved to meet Terra's as she went by.

She didn't acknowledge him.

Ben however, noticed his stare. Catching Brent's eye he tipped his chin, and suddenly Brent wondered if he'd seen this coming.

As he watched them leave, he sensed a presence drawing near to him. Twisting his head in the other direction, he saw that Ivan was approaching.

The giant regarded both Brent and his friends with a grave look. "Watch Renée," he told them, his tone gruffer at this lower volume, and he walked through the yammering crowd and back outside, calling for the villagers to disperse.

Lowering his eyes from the chief, Brent pivoted to view the sparring arena.

Renée was standing right where Terra had left her. But instead of staring after her mother, she'd switched to thinly smiling between the villagers who'd come to congratulate her on her victory.

But beneath her grateful façade, Brent could tell that she was just barely hiding her concern.

"Renée!" Mekial broke away from the thinning crowd and ran to her. "That was —!"

"Unreal!" someone else burst over him and Mekial whipped around as Tyre and Kro came into view.

It was Tyre who'd spoken. "Talk about unexpected!" he said as he got closer. "You just kicked your mom!"

"In the *face!*" Kro added, leaning on Renée's shoulder. In front of them Brent, Aaron, Liam, Harver and Eklaire joined their circle. "The village is never gonna stop talking about it!"

"I know…" Renée dropped her head, dismay overtaking her. "I hope she's okay…"

"C'mon, it's *Terra,*" Kro said, rising to his full height. "She's been through worse, right?"

"I'm sure she's fine," Tyre waved a hand. "I mean, if you were a slave trader, she definitely would've jumped up and flipped you over her shoulder or something. But I think she took that kick like a man."

"Stuck it out —"

"Admitted defeat —"

"Like a good loser," Kro finished.

Renée frowned.

"Ya'll shouldn't be so cold!" Eklaire piped up, her nearly invisible eyebrows drawing together. "That kick looked like a real doozy! Terra might be out of it fer a while!"

"In the end, Renée at least proved herself, right?" Kro countered. "Wasn't that the point of all this?"

"Not to mention they were fighting with real weapons." Tyre shrugged. "I mean, somebody was *bound* to get clobbered."

Eklaire's frown deepened.

"He has a point, Eklaire," Liam said.

Eklaire's heterochromatic eyes leaped to his face urgently. Then, with a slight drop of her shoulders, they fell to the floor.

"'Course I do!" Tyre held out a hand out for Liam to slap.

Liam stared at him.

Still grinning, Tyre slapped it himself.

"Don't worry, Renée. I'm sure she's fine," Kro continued carelessly. "She totally ate that kick."

"Yeah. With her face." Harver raised a sarcastic eyebrow.

"You know what I mean."

Renée turned away, stung by Harver's words.

Brent noticed. "Ben's probably taking Terra up to Khirsta's hut," he told her and at the mention of the village's head healer, Renée looked up at him. "They might be there by now."

"You gonna go see 'em?" Eklaire asked and without even a moment's thought, Renée nodded.

"Yeah," she said, and her gaze panned across the others' faces. "I'll just…catch up with you guys later."

"I'll come, too!" Mekial cried as Renée went to retrieve her sword. "Bye, guys!" he called to the others, waving his arms over his head.

As the pair headed for the doors, Brent watched Renée closely. It wasn't at all difficult for him to see the distracted anxiety that lingered upon her brow.

A soft line of worry creased his own and he wondered if a deeper meaning had been hidden in Ivan's request.

47

FOR THE REST of the day, Renée was nowhere to be found. Although many of the villagers could confess that they'd spotted her here and there, none could testify as to where she'd gone next. His friends didn't either. Not even Mekial knew where she was.

Brent was sure that he knew every part of the village, and along with that every place that his friends would go if they'd ambled off alone. But still, he couldn't find her.

In time, a number of assignments and requests from the villagers came up, keeping him from exacting her location. There were a few meetings with the auction raiders that he had to attend, after which Rufus had him come along and visit the newcomers, just to see how they were adjusting to life in Taranis after their late-night rescue. Though they'd barely been in Taranis for half a day, finding out that almost half of them hadn't made it out of the raid in Heletica's Pass had probably overwhelmed them. Add to that the news about a girl fighting her own mother, and it was likely that they felt this "sanctuary" wasn't what they'd thought it would be.

Quelling their concerns wasn't arduous, fortunately: just knowing that they were far from the Empire and that the village leadership was willing to help them settle in was enough.

Shortly after this, some of the engineers had him test out a new piece of equipment that could break chains and prison bars in one blow, if a raider was without the help of an aetherist. Brent's feedback left them excitedly swapping ideas for the next prototype.

After that, his day only got busier: from helping a villager fix his broken drum to refereeing a round of Mud Ball for some trainees, he ended up being drawn into odd-jobs by nearly everyone. Even Greta enlisted his help, for she needed some very specific culinary herbs from the far reaches of the valley.

Liam went with him, and on finding the requested ingredients they learned that they were under the protection of a very angry pack of dicani who were raising their cubs in a nearby den.

After fending the wild canines off, the raiders let them keep their territory. They'd only needed the ingredients, anyway.

Upon their return, Greta had met them with a little face that was bright with gratitude. "I wouldn't have been able to get any of these myself," she said, accepting the supplies. "How lucky I am to have such strong young men readily available."

Brent grinned. "Anytime, Greta."

"Careful," Liam warned. "She'll hold you to it."

"Aw, she's worth it."

"I wanna see where you got her herbs from!" Lilian exclaimed. "Grandma says there's big yellow beetles in the caves near them. I wanna see!"

"Maybe after the dicani move out, Lil," Liam told her. "Wouldn't want you to get hurt."

"Awww…but you guys just beat 'em up, didn't you? Can't we go back now?"

"No. 'Sides" — Liam looked at Brent — "Uncle Brent's got someplace he needs to be."

Brent blinked. "I do?"

"Ren's probably home by now," Liam said plainly and he nodded up at the sky, which had darkened on their way back to the village. Stars glittered across it and the moon had long-since manifested. "Lot happened for her today. She prob'ly just needed some space."

"I saw Auntie Ren!" Lilian suddenly cried, jumping up and down. "She was with Lady Xëri while you guys were gone and then she, uh…" She thought for a second. "Oh yeah! She went to the Main House!"

"Now that's some solid intel!" Brent knelt before the girl, who grinned. "Keep that up, and you might even take your uncle's job someday."

Liam huffed at this, his arms folding. But the smirk on his face as he looked at his niece was one of pride.

She giggled.

"Thanks, squirt." Brent pinched Lilian's nose and got to his feet.

"Mekial said Auntie Ren's been feeling down," she remembered as he started off and she pointed at him with a frown. "So be nice!"

Turning, he smiled at her. "Don't worry. I will."

Lowering her hand the child smiled back, pleased.

And so, they parted.

Much to Brent's surprise, he ended up crossing paths with Renée much sooner than he'd expected: halfway to the Main House, she came walking towards him with her head bowed in thought.

A breeze caught her hair as she walked, sweeping loose strands away from her pinched face. Holding the rest of it back, she raised her head to look up at the sky.

She caught sight of Brent instead, and stopped. "Brent!"

The side of his mouth rose into a half-smile, and the knot of concern that had once been tight in his chest at last came loose. "There you are."

Upon inquiry, she explained that she was on her way to the valley river. Brent offered to accompany her and when they reached the riverbank, she tilted her head back and gazed at the moon.

Brent slid her a sidelong look before following her line of sight.

The silence between them was heavy, thick, and it lasted just a bit longer than he was comfortable with.

He broke it. "So."

Renée didn't respond, her eyes still heavenward.

Brent rocked on the balls of his feet for a second. Straightening up casually, he made another attempt. "Looked like you were thinkin' pretty hard about something back there."

"I…yeah." Renée lowered her head and, gathering her hair into one hand, she pulled it over her shoulder. "I was thinking…"

Brent waited, but when it seemed that she'd clearly retreated into her thoughts again, he offered a nudge. "'Bout what?"

Renée glanced up at him and then, stroking her hair, she dropped her gaze to the river. "I was just thinking about…how much I take a lot of things here for granted."

He frowned. "How?"

"I helped with the new villagers earlier," she began. "A lot of them were saying that they were…overwhelmed. They just couldn't believe that they're really safe now." She released her hair and looked up at the moon again. She was quiet for a moment. "I was also thinking about how, now that I'm able to keep training, the world suddenly seems…different."

Brent held his tongue, waiting for her to go on.

"The reality of what I've decided to do since I was small… it hadn't completely set in until today." Her eyes dropped to the horizon, beyond the mountains that faded into the distance. "It's as if finally getting my mom's approval, and then meeting the people you guys saved right after…it suddenly made everything clear." Her face changed, her eyebrows arching with unease. "I actually listened to some of their stories this time. And not like how when I was younger, and there were certain things that I just…couldn't under-stand. But I actually, really listened. And…I heard about the slaves who didn't make it back." The crease in her brow deepened, and her gaze became more remote as she envisioned the world that laid beyond the valley. "The Empire…is a lot more evil than I'd once thought it was. Isn't it?"

Coming out of herself, she looked at Brent.

But he wasn't looking at her anymore. Instead, he'd lowered his eyes to the river.

She wondered what he was thinking. "Was it difficult for you, too?" she asked at last. "To adjust to life here, I mean."

He laughed dryly and looked at her. "Yeah."

She eyed him carefully and when she next spoke, her voice was still cautious. "You don't really…talk about it very much."

Brent glanced aside, and the movement of his eyebrows implied agreement. He'd never spoken a word about how he'd felt during his own transition, much less what he was transitioning from.

And to be honest, he didn't want to.

"It is overwhelming, I can say that much," he admitted. "But, you learn to get used to it over time." He flashed her a quick smile before looking away. But as he continued, his expression became more and more detached. "It gets easier after a while. You don't jump at the same things. Or twist people's words around…"

Renée's face saddened.

Brent noticed and he laughed lightly, almost guiltily. "C'mon, Ren, you don't need to look so upset. It's no big deal."

Her brow crinkled even more. "But…"

"Really, Ren. I'm fine. That stuff doesn't happen anymore." He smiled. "And I stopped by to visit the new villagers today, too. They'll see the truth soon enough. Just give 'em time."

She smiled back, but it wasn't very believable.

He decided to change the subject. "Anyway, how're you holdin' up?"

"Huh?" She blinked, not sure what he meant.

"I mean with your match against your mom. You practically disappeared afterwards." What resolution that he'd displayed earlier faded to allow for honest concern. "Are you okay?"

"Oh. Well," she smiled sheepishly, "it's not every day you kick your mom in the face and everyone's okay with it. But, I'm all right," she added when he seemed to search her face for some underlying emotion. "I got to talk to her and, well, I guess you could say she wasn't very happy about it but, she's really letting me keep going. She even said that she wants to teach me how to kick harder." She laughed quietly.

Brent's face softened. "Guess she's holding up fine."

Renée nodded. "Just knowing that she approves of my skill… it means a lot." She looked away, smiling to herself. "Taranis isn't all that old, y'know? Mom was one of the first female raiders in all of the Liberation Fronts. It kind of feels like I'm following in the footsteps of a legend."

It was Brent's turn to laugh this time. "You make it sound like she's dead. Or retired."

"Oh." Renée looked guilty.

"Nah, don't sweat it. I'm sure she'd appreciate it. Y'know, if she was dead. Or retired."

Renée shook her head, though her lips were traced with the

smallest of smiles. A moment later, it became genuine. "Thank you," she said. "For asking, I mean."

"No problem." He glanced at the night sky. "Anyway, we should probably start heading back. The night watch is starting and it's getting late. We don't wanna be around when some wild animals decide to come out here looking for dinner." His eyes widened, horrified by something that he could see over her shoulder. "Like those right there — oh, no, *Renée, watch out!*"

Renée actually panicked and ran into his arms, her long hair swinging as she looked back.

There was nothing there.

Brent chuckled gently, cradling her figure as he smiled down at her.

Renée looked up hastily, then pushed him away. *"Brent!"*

He laughed openly. "You just make it so easy!" He pretended to jump at her. *"Ahh!"*

She stiffened. Closing her eyes, she calmed herself.

Brent kept laughing.

Renée sighed and, though knowledge of his joke was plain in the curve of her mouth, she started up the road. "It's been a long day," she said. "Think I should probably get to bed."

Brent's eyes followed her for a second before he allowed himself a question. "Are you mad?"

"No." She kept walking.

It was a candid response, certainly. But her gait was out of character: her arms were crossed, her shoulders were squared, and her steps matched the cadence of a quiet march.

"Really?" Brent caught up with her easily, then turned so that he was walking backwards next to her. "Cuz…you seem mad."

Her teeth flashed at him quickly, a gentle light in the darkness. "I'm not mad, Brent. But I did leave my sword, and if something does come out, I wouldn't want to be caught defenseless."

This time, it was Brent's teeth that met the dark, if only briefly. "Fair point. But I've got *my* swords." Reaching up he gripped his bladed staff, which was still holstered to his back after his mission with Liam. "And you don't *really* think I'd just stand there and panic if something was gonna try and eat you, do you?"

He saw the tension in her shoulders loosen and she stopped walking, which led him to do the same. He stood over her.

"Probably not," she admitted, her face tilted towards his.

She was standing close again, so much so that they could feel each other's warmth.

It was an enveloping heat, Brent felt, but not one that was overwhelming. Rather, it brought ease and calm after a day that had been rich with activity.

He'd never been one to mind the busier days. But, in this particular moment, to have a chance to pause with her was —

Something crashed on the opposite side of the road, piercing the night with the clatter of wood and a soft gasp of surprise.

Startled, the two looked up.

Kurt was on the other side of the stream, and was just now picking up the bundle of firewood that he'd dropped. The stack that was set up beside his family's cabin was ample; he appeared to have taken too many logs at once.

Glancing up, he spotted the pair. "Oh! Hi, guys!"

"'Sup, Kurt." Brent lifted a hand in greeting.

"Do you need help?" Renée called, noticing he was struggling.

"All good!" With a quiet grunt and one final adjustment, he jogged away. "Night!" He vanished around the corner of his home.

As he went, Brent chanced to look at Renée again.

She passed him a wordless smile at the same time. When she circled him to approach the front steps of her own abode, he stepped back with a quiet, near silent, clearing of his throat.

"Thanks for walking me home," she said when she'd reached the door. With her hand on the knocker, she looked back at him. "See you tomorrow?"

"Yeah." The lantern that marked her home added an extra glow to his eyes. "For sure."

She smiled. Then with a flip of her hair and a push of the door, she was gone.

Brent didn't linger. Turning away, he went to continue up the hill and head home.

He was nearly there when the wind touched him, kicking leaves and dirt into the air. His hair shook and he squinted, his golden eyes narrowing against the gust, and he was forced to stop when it picked up speed.

At the same time his ears shivered, latching onto a quiet growl that was cradled inside of it.

His eyebrows twitched with confusion and his arm went up to guard his sight. As for his eyes they flashed painlessly, glinting like starlight as a teal-colored glow washed over them —

Then, all at once, everything stopped.

And the air vibrated. Like it was buzzing.

Lowering his arm Brent looked around, and his eyes grew large.

Taranis was gone, and the world was now suffused with gentle clouds of teal, and gold, and white. The sky was reflected in the ground, clear and open, and all around him the air continued to tremble, to buzz.

To hum.

"You…"

Brent spiraled and the mists parted, unveiling a quiet figure that stood several paces behind him. Their sky-blue hair twirled delicately, lifted by the winds that still breezed about, and the ends of their ornamented cloak fluttered.

Words left Brent before he could stop himself: "You again…"

The man heard him — the way his head rose slightly was a sign.

Brent froze.

"Can you," the man started to turn, but even when his face circled into view the glowing lights of this otherworldly plane extended across it, *"see me?"*

Brent hesitated. He didn't say anything else.

"In that case," the man's soft tone of surprise gave way to severity, *"the distortions must be —"*

Brent blinked.

The roads of Taranis were empty.

As far as he could tell there was no one and nothing else around: no man surrounded by strange clouds, no clear and open sky, no shallow pool of water that mirrored existence. All was normal. Calm. Even his eyes had reverted to their natural color, though he hadn't at all noticed their initial change.

In every sense, everything was quiet. And he was alone. *tv*

ANOTHER WORLD
CODE: DISTORTION

Terra was sitting in the dining room when Renée walked inside. Perfectly still, she balanced the edge of her mug atop the table and swirled it gently.

She didn't look up. "Sit down, Ren."

Renée closed the door. Bracing herself, she took a deep breath and sat down across from her mother. She hadn't expected her to be awake.

Her eyes flicked to the woman's cheek.

The bandage that Khirsta had set there was still secure. It hid the purpling bruise that Renée had given her quite nicely.

"How is it?" she asked, feeling a bit awkward. "Your…face."

Terra cracked a small smile, but her eyes remained distant. "I've dealt with worse."

"Ah. Right."

"I wanted to let you know…that I'm proud of you. And of what you pulled off today." Terra took some of her drink. The candlelight showed it to be water that had been purified in one of the clay pots in the kitchen. "It's not very often someone manages to kick me in the head like that."

"Th…thank you." Renée sat up a bit straighter. "…I think."

"There's room for improvement." Terra finished the rest of her water and looked at Renée over the rim of her cup. Her dark eyes were hard.

She seemed to be thinking.

Renée pressed her lips together.

Terra put her cup down. Her eyes were on it now.

"…I need to share something with you," she said at length. "Something about my fighting style that only a few people know."

"Right — those kicks!" Renée perked up. "What was that? I've never seen you do that before!"

"It's something that I learned a long time ago." Terra looked up. "Most of the villagers that I've fought beside have seen it. Even when I explain it to them they don't fully understand it. But I'm going to tell you now…there's a distinction that needs to be made."

There was confusion in Renée's eyes. But, she decided against announcing it.

"The aether…is a complex thing." Terra grabbed hold of her mug and tilted it. Without truly focusing on it, she gazed into its depths. "As you know, aetheriests can use it to manipulate the elements, disappear, or even move things without touching them. But you can do a lot more with it than that. Even without it."

Leaning forward, she planted her mug in the middle of the table.

Renée stared at it for a second, and then her.

"Channel your quintessence properly," Terra sat back down, "and you can demonstrate a show of physical force that's not possible for any human. Not even for aetheriests."

"What —?"

Terra flicked the mug.

The air popped and a sharp blast of wind hit Renée in the face, throwing her hair and accessories back —

The mug went zooming past her cheek like an arrow, ripped across the room, and smashed to pieces against the wall.

Renée spun in her chair to see it, wide-eyed.

Thunderstruck, she rounded on her mother.

"That's how I fight when I'm dealing with the imperials." Folding her arms Terra looked her dead in the eye, as if what she'd done had been rather boring. "The downside is that you need to get up close and personal with your opponent. But if you play your cards right, even that can get easier. At that point, breaking bones, armor or even grappling a soldier is no hard thing. But it takes practice."

"So you…" Renée fit it all together. "You're an aetheriest?"

"Not necessarily. What I do requires a more instinctual connection with the aether. Heldar and the others have different methods. We're not the same."

"Still, you…" Renée frowned. "What about Mekial? With all the things he's been able to do since he was a kid, he has to be an aetheriest."

"Like I said: it's different. And Mekial's quintessence seems… sporadic. Not even Heldar really knows what to do with him.

"But right now, I'm more concerned about you." Terra held her daughter's eyes. "Empyrean's Guard is one of the Liberation Front's biggest threats right now, and they've had a lot of success over the last few years. Not only with ending riots and uprisings in the Empire, but also with razing a number of our sister villages to the ground.

"The way that I fight, and the way that most of our raiders fight, gives each of us a number of advantages when we meet imperials out in the field. I stand by what I said: I won't get in the way of your graduating into Taranis' ranks. But," her eyes gained a certain sharpness, "I still think that putting you in the imperials' crosshairs would be irresponsible."

Renée flinched, stung.

"Tomorrow," Terra got out of her seat, "I'll go to the chief and have you added to Leonard's team."

"Leonard…?!" Renée's growing eyes watched as Terra started out of the dining room, and her limbs trembled with anger. "Leonard already has his team: he's the strategist, and he already has a designated intel scout and recon scout!"

"You'll be their support."

"I'll be at *home!*" Renée objected, and she sprang to her feet. "If I'm not at least assigned to be a scout on someone's team, I'll only ever be on missions once in a blue moon!"

"That's fine with me."

"But not with me!"

Terra's face became as flat as stone.

"I didn't train under Jeffrey since I was six years old just to sit at home," Renée argued. "I did it so that I could help you and the other raiders out in the field! But if you're so worried that I'm not ready for it, then *you* train me! Teach me what you just did" — she glanced back at the broken mug as an indication — "teach me how to fight like you do!"

Terra was silent.

Renée was the same, and she held her mother with a firm glare paired with straight shoulders.

After a moment, Terra sighed. She folded her arms again. "Even if it's not as flashy as what Heldar and the other aetheriests do, what I just showed you still requires a good grasp of the aether and quintessence overall. You can't learn it in a day."

"Then take more than a day to train me! You never showed any fear of my being a raider until you heard about Empyrean's Guard," Renée pointed out. "But *you* still go into the Empire and fight! Even if I never get the chance to join anyone on a raid, what would I do if Empyrean's Guard ended up coming here next?"

Terra's eyes flinched.

Renée's were downcast. "If I really am as unprepared as you think, I wouldn't have any choice but to be a victim at that point." She looked her mother in the eye again. "And that would be just as irresponsible!"

The resolution in Terra's expression wavered, and she looked away.

"I proved myself to you today," Renée reminded her. "I passed your test, and everyone else in the village knows that I'm just as good of a fighter as anyone else. I know it, too.

"But if you think I'm still lacking," she pressed, "if there's the smallest chance that you think that I could end up hurt, or worse — then teach me to be like you. Teach me to be stronger."

Terra's eyes snapped up to her.

Renée was sincere.

It was no wonder: both of her parents had been an inspiration to her. She'd always wanted to be as strong as they were. To protect, to fight, to stand firm and oppose injustice, even at the threat of death like they did, and all for the benefit of others...

She would do whatever it took to reach that point. To prove to her mother that she was just as capable of joining their cause.

Terra didn't speak at all. In fact, the entire room was gripped by her silence.

At long last, she nodded. Lifting her head out of her thoughts, she rested her full attention upon her daughter. "Fine," she said.

Renée's eyesbrows rose as her shock settled in.

"We'll start in the morning." Terra circled, meaning to head to her room.

"R..." Renée hastened to wrap her mind around what had just happened. "Really?"

Terra looked at her over her shoulder. "Did I stutter?"

Slowly but surely, Renée grinned.

"You're a lot more like me than I've been willing to admit, Renée." Terra's thoughts wandered, taking her gaze along with them. "When you set your mind on something you go for it, tooth and nail. Looking at it like that, it's no wonder we've butt heads over this so many times. But you made a fair point: if I'm gonna let you fight, I might as well teach you everything I know to make sure you don't get captured. Or die.

"What I'm going to teach you is something that was passed down to me," she went on and she faced her, "by someone who was almost like my mother. Feels like it was forever ago now."

Her hand wandered over to the black-and-red bracer that was latched to her right forearm. The emblem atop it, which resembled a glowing flame, was cold to the touch.

"…Maybe I'll share that story with you sometime," she added quietly.

At that, Renée found herself eyeing her mother with wonder. She'd never seen her offer such vulnerability before.

"Anyway, get some sleep." Dropping her arm, Terra started down the hall. "You're gonna need it."

Renée stood up straight, her eyes shining. "Yes, ma'am!"

✙

When Foedia entered the imperial study, she was surprised to find the emperor there, sitting before the fire with his hands tightly laced before him. Dressed in his gold-trimmed tunic, golden jewelry and his hair styled into a loose braid, he was as stiff as a statue. She wondered if he was praying?

She'd never seen the emperor pray before, but she did suspect that he was one of the most religious men that she'd ever known. His belief in the imperial gods Empyrean and Vedrah seemed to surpass that of anyone she'd ever met in her life. Then again, given his situation — and hers — she couldn't imagine his faith being otherwise.

But, from what she'd seen of his actions, it didn't seem as if he harbored any reverence for either of the deities. In fact, whenever he crossed paths with any of their manmade depictions, he seemed to regard them with a strange level of contempt…and fear.

Moving softly, she circled the furniture so as to not disturb him. Drifting around to the side of the couch that he was sitting on, she tried to see if he was indeed praying.

He wasn't. His golden eyes were open and pinned to the fires.

In a flash, his gaze shifted to her.

Foedia's heart leaped. She retreated. "I beg your pardon, Your Majesty. I didn't mean to sneak up on you."

Koberius slowly turned from her to review the fires once more. "Nothing can sneak up on me," he said quietly. "Not when" — he winced and his fingers flew for his left eye. But the pain receded quickly, so he relaxed — "not when this spirit resides in my body, watching even what I can't."

Foedia nodded thoughtfully, but didn't speak.

Koberius passed her another sidelong look. "…You're yourself again, I see."

"Majesty?"

"Your aura. Your manner. It's all different." He stared into the fire. "Normally when I see you it's Vedrah's company I get to entertain. But I suppose, like Empyrean, he's decided to withdraw for now." He closed his eyes with a sort of pale smirk. "A strange change of pace, to say the least."

The woman didn't know how to respond to that. So, she didn't.

"Do you ever wonder of fate, Foedia?" the emperor asked her at length.

"Majesty?"

"Everything I do…and everything I've ever done…every action, every thought…" Unclenching his hands, Koberius looked at them.

They were shaking.

Curling them into fists, he took on the same pose that he'd been in when Foedia had arrived. "If I'd been born into any other family, maybe even at a different time…I wonder what I'd be today. I can no longer tell what's mine, and what's his. At first there was a time when I could see the distinction, but now…even in this moment, I wonder who I am. What I am."

Foedia waited.

"Is it the same for you?" Koberius looked at her. "Like me, this path was chosen for you. You had no say. Do you still feel it now? That with every passing day, you lose more of yourself to what's taken residence inside you."

Foedia turned aside. She nodded quietly.

"And I'm the one who robbed you of that choice."

Foedia looked at him.

Koberius was sitting up. His usually hard face was softer now. "I even gave you your name. And I doubt it's the same one that your parents gave you."

"…I don't have parents, Your Majesty. My past isn't one particularly worth remembering…the rest of my memories are tied to living at the Shrine of Astria, as one her Daughters."

Koberius didn't react.

Foedia continued. "As for whether or not I had a choice, I did: I volunteered. When I heard about what you wanted. To serve the emperor who houses Empyrean…is an honor."

Koberius was silent.

"Is that you," he finally asked, "or is that Vedrah speaking right now?"

Foedia looked up sharply.

"You were terrified that day." Koberius got to his feet and slowly crossed the room towards her. "I could feel it. We both could. Empyrean…and myself." He stopped rather close to her. If she'd wanted to, she could've reached out and embraced him.

Koberius' face was deadpan when he next spoke, and it made his words that much more unsettling. "We fed on it."

Foedia swallowed.

Without warning, Koberius snatched her by the cheek and tilted her face up to him. The firelight danced across her grotesque, scaly skin.

"Would your mother recognize you now, I wonder?" He stroked her rough cheek with his thumb.

Suddenly he let go of her, as if her skin had burned him. His lips drew back to reveal a smile, but his eyes were sad. "This assignment was forced onto us both. And neither one of us can get out of it. Not until the gods themselves are satisfied…or freer than we are now. And we both know what that means."

Foedia didn't speak.

With his face falling, Koberius turned and marched for the door.

"Your Majesty —" Foedia began.

"Don't allow yourself to think that you have any control," the emperor said, turning to look at her with those piercing, golden eyes. "Not even on the days where it seems that your mind is your own. The sooner you accept that, the better. Then perhaps when we are both granted freedom, it could mean that much more."

He left.

48

S HORT OF BREATH, *Brent ran down the marble halls of the manor as fast as his thin legs could carry him. Around him the walls shifted, their smooth faces gleaming like fire, and clouds of smoke crawled at his feet. The eyes of portraits were glued to him as he went by, their stoic faces catching the glow of drifting embers, and shadows writhed and snaked behind him, swallowing the hall at one end while he desperately fled for the other.*

The air was unbearably hot. It made his throat sting, dried out his eyes. And it felt heavy — it was as if something was sitting on top of him, pressing down on his small shoulders to slow his gait.

He tried ignoring it. Pumping his skinny arms, he tried to outrun the sensation of being watched, of being suffocated by a mass that he couldn't see — a mass that he knew wasn't aetherial. But its presence only grew, magnifying until he could feel it on all sides of his body. It made the hair of his nape stand on end.

Something like a voice hissed in his ears, sending cold shivers shooting down his back. He couldn't tell where it was coming from, only that he could hear it from everywhere all at once. Its words were unintelligible at first, drifting out as meaningless sighs.

Then, finally, its jumbled sneers gathered into a single word:
"You…"

He kept running, gasping heavily, his arms like lead. Every breath brought with it a short stab of pain that knifed his throat, stabbed his chest.

The portraits watched him unblinkingly. Red light raged across the walls, flashing like fire. Burnt banners and broken pillars toppled around him, sending his mind into a panic. He ran faster.

"You…"

He started wheezing.

"You…!"

Kicking out, he wheeled around a corner.

Immediately a boy's face met him, his eyes cursed with a horrible kind of asymmetry: one was narrow and gold while the other was large and reptilian. A long, vertical slit stretched from his eyelid to the water-line.

Brent swore he stopped breathing.

"It's you…" The boy's face lacked emotion, but the intensity of his stare was unholy.

He was older than Brent, with flying, indigo-blue hair and a golden crown made of gilded leaves and eagle's wings. The train of his robes stretched into the abysmal darkness that surrounded him, and along with his presence there existed a peculiar pressure in the air. It was the same as in the halls from before but it was worse here, more tangible. Brent could almost feel a pair of spindly claws winding around his shoulders, as if the invisible weight was manifesting some kind of infernal body.

"You did it…"

Fire blazed around the boy, and at the same time his only normal eye popped and bulged to match the other.

"You tainted my bloodline…" The boy reached out for Brent, his fingers curling like claws. "With Zion's blood…!"

With one hand, he snatched Brent's face.

All at once Brent's eyes popped open, and he shot up in bed with a startled shout.

Almost immediately, his bedroom door slammed open and Xëri all but flew inside. "What's wrong?!"

Brent blinked, staring at her foggily until he came back to his senses. "N…nothing," he managed. "Nightmare…"

"Oh." Xëri relaxed, but her concern was still visible. "You haven't had nightmares in a while."

"Yeah." Brent sniffed, thumbed his nose. He didn't look at her.

"Weird."

Xëri's brow furrowed worriedly. "Why don't you come out and eat?" she suggested. "I've got breakfast ready. Ivan's already left to help with preparations for the Feast, and Aaron and I were going to go and help out after eating."

"Yeah." Brent rubbed his face and swung his legs over the side of his bed. "I'll be out."

Xëri regarded him for a second longer before leaving him to his privacy.

Leaning forward, Brent raked his hands through his hair.

He'd told Renée that it didn't bother him anymore. That he was fine.

But it still haunted him.

Running his hands down the back of his neck, he closed his eyes and sighed.

The past would always be with him, wouldn't it?

And not only that…

Glimpses of the strange vision that he'd had the previous night entered his head: clouds of gold and green; the man with sky-blue hair who'd spoken to him…

He'd spoken to Brent, hadn't he?

He rubbed his face.

What was that about?

"They say Zion the Hero was a brooding recluse sometimes."

Brent looked at the door.

Aaron was leaning against the frame, munching on a breakfast of hard-boiled eggs and roasted steak.

Shaking his head, he took another bite of his food. "Doesn't really suit you much."

Brent cracked a smile. "Right. Being a mopey grump is more your style, *iytamhal.*" He got up right as Aaron frowned at him.

The redhead ate a bit more of his breakfast. "You still got that look on your face."

"What look?" Approaching his dresser, Brent tossed on his jade necklace and snatched up his armlet.

"The 'mopey grump' look."

Brent nodded admittedly and slipped his armlet on. His face

was serious. "…I've been having weird dreams lately."

"No kidding."

"These are different." Brent frowned at nothing. "When I graduated last year, remember how I told you I went to Adelle's grave?"

"Yeah, and then you said you heard some weird sound."

"That's not all that happened," Brent admitted. "I saw someone. He was standing in this green fog, or something."

"Definitely sounds like a weird dream."

"Except I was awake. And it happened again last night, when I was on my way home. Think *he* saw *me* this time, too."

Aaron stared at him. His bright eyes twitched as he mulled it all over. "Why didn't you mention something before?"

"I hadn't really thought about it much, 'til we ran into that guy in Cleopa. And with it happening again yesterday, well…"

"What's this about green mist?" Xëri appeared in the hallway, having come from one of the back rooms after storing some kitchen items there.

"Just this dream I keep having," Brent told her. "Or…not-a-dream. I keep seeing the same guy, in the same green and yellow mist."

"Green and…?" Xëri narrowed her eyes for a second. She seemed skeptical. "What does this 'guy' look like?"

Brent shrugged. "It's hard to see him. Just…really long hair, some sorta cloak. Can never see his face, though."

"Long hair?"

"Yeah." Brent thought for a second. "It actually looks like mine. The color, I mean."

Xëri paused and became unnaturally quiet. "…How long have you been having this dream?"

"Only twice." Brent glanced over at Aaron, as if to determine whether or not he, too, could sense the peculiarity of Xëri's behavior. He could. "Once when I graduated. And again just yesterday."

Xëri turned away, thinking.

"Why? You heard of him or something?"

"No…" Xëri slowly returned to the present moment, and she glanced between the boys with a rather pale smile. "Of course not. It was your dream, remember?"

"Does the Elder's daughter live here in Taranis?" Aaron blurted.

Xëri raised her eyebrows, completely surprised. Her voice remained level. "What makes you ask that?"

"When we were coming back from our mission in Dukaris," Brent relayed to her, "we had a run-in with some guy in a half-mask that looked like a lion. He said a lot of crazy stuff before saying that the Elder's daughter would be able to tell us more."

"Ah, right. Your father mentioned that. It sounded like that man knows a lot about the Liberation Fronts as a whole."

"Think it's bad news for us?" Aaron asked pointedly, straightening against the doorframe. He held Xëri's eyes with his own.

Xëri offered him a kind, gentle smile instead of the troubled look he'd been expecting. She rubbed his arm. "We can only hope. Right?" She looked between them.

The boys didn't respond.

"So, the Elder's daughter..." Brent tried again.

"I don't know." Xëri's lips were pressed into another smile of false cheer. "The Elder was involved in the founding of the Liberation Fronts. But I've heard that he likes his secrets; I haven't got much to share about his family."

Aaron and Brent exchanged looks.

"Well, if that's all." Xëri patted Aaron's shoulder and smiled at Brent. It was genuine this time. "We'd better get going if we want tonight's Feast to go well!" Lifting the hem of her dress, she started for the door. "I guess I'll see you boys down there! Brent, your food's already on the table!"

She left.

"Well?" Brent looked at Aaron who pushed away from the doorframe.

He dumped his fork into his bowl with a bright-eyed scowl. "She's lying."

⚘

"...That said, reports have been coming in from Varrone that the newly founded 'Katruskik Alliance' has staged an attack on the locals, stripping them of livestock and other supplies. No kidnappings or deaths were reported, but there were many casualties." The royal advisor unrolled one of the scrolls that were stacked in front of him and scanned its initial paragraphs, reading the Arkanian script from top to bottom, right to left. "The citizens of Varrone are requesting medicine and other supplies for the wounded, as well as financial support for damages and the replenishing of their trade products.

"If they're not able to provide for the market by the end of the month, other towns ringing Lyrik's western border will find themselves under certain financial strains as well. They won't be as steep as what Varrone is struggling with, but if we move quickly we can mitigate the economic repercussions that will likely occur." He set the scroll down and looked across the long, black marble table that extended in front of him.

Directly opposite him sat Viceroy Diomedes, his dark face lined with few wrinkles and his once saturated, navy hair having grayed a little. The ruler sighed heavily and, lifting a hand, he rubbed his short, evenly trimmed beard.

Soon resting his hands on the table he looked between the men and women who sat with him. Clothed in embroidered togas and dresses of blue satin trimmed with gold, they joined him in this wide conference room of Lyrik Estate, which was a stone room with a balcony just behind the provincial ruler. Rounded columns edged either wall.

Their meeting had begun shortly after sunrise. By now, the light of day had brightened and the angle of the shadows had shifted. It seemed hours had gone by, perhaps more than what Diomedes had originally budgeted for the meeting.

Not that that was surprising. It only meant that he'd have a much shorter break between this gathering and the next one.

He rubbed his face wearily. "How many attacks does this make so far?"

"Nine, sir," the same advisor replied. "Within the last two months. They've become rather bold lately."

"And less than two months ago I was told that these rebels

would keep their fighting limited to the military presence in Brusseir," Diomedes said tensely. "Or, at the least, that Empyrean's Guard would *keep* them in Brusseir. And now they're bleeding into my territory."

"Yes, my lord," the advisor continued worriedly. "Viceroy Damokles did give us his sworn word that he would keep the rebels in check, but…"

"There's no need to sugarcoat it. My younger brother has never been one for being able to rein in chaos when he thrives on embodying it himself." Diomedes leaned back in his chair as he spoke of the provincial ruler of Brusseir. The man certainly was unruly in character, and as cumbersome as it was Diomedes wasn't entirely surprised by his lax grip on the Katruskik rebels. "Have Ilkanos look into the budget and see how much we can afford to send to the people of Varrone. Then, have the soldiers at the outpost north of Axelius dispatch a unit to inspect the caves of Mount Julius and any other leads that the locals may have on where the rebels may be hiding. I'll not have Damokles' indifference ruin my jurisdiction.

"Any of the Katruskik rebels found are to be promptly brought to the execution grounds. That goes for whether they're located in Varrone, or elsewhere. Make a note of it, and arrange for couriers to deliver the message throughout the capital and the surrounding towns," he added, nodding to the royal secretary sitting near him.

She quickly scribbled down his instructions.

Picking up the handkerchief that was sitting in front of him, Diomedes coughed into it roughly. "What's next?"

"Empyrean's Guard is still working actively to uncover the savages who continue to assault the slave trade," another advisor spoke up. "Skylok, Blaze and the Silver Shadow remain at large."

"So there's no change."

"Not since the guardsmen discovered that abominable goblin-village in the lowlands west of Orinn, Your Highness," another woman replied. "What's more is that one of them, Skylok in particular, has begun to gain widespread attention from the public as demands for its arrest spread across the province. It's starting some unsightly rumors."

"Yes, I know of them," Diomedes replied evenly. "They suspect that Skylok is somehow related to the royal family."

"Yes. So, consequently, they suspect that the Empire is working against itself to undermine the slave trade," the advisor added crossly. "This cannot stand. Your Highness, you're the viceroy of Lyrik Province and, more recently, you have become the crown prince of the Empire, what with His Imperial Majesty still lacking an heir and the passing of Viceroy Atticus, father of Viceroy Antony, two years ago. Since Skylok appears to be solely active in this province, I urge you to make a statement denouncing its impossible relationship to the royal family."

Diomedes considered this with a troubled scowl.

"The gossips' justification for these rumors is troublesome as well, sire," a young man sitting near him piped up, earning his attention. "Only the imperial royal family is known for possessing traits such as yours. Blue hair and golden eyes are nonexistent in Lenora Province, although the people there are known for having a vast array of colorful phenotypes. So —"

"And yet, there is not one person in the imperial royal family that possesses the traits of an Avat," the viceroy returned sharply, and the young man clamped his mouth shut. "Do not rub salt into an old wound, Minister Phoebus. My son died almost a decade ago, in a terrible accident that nearly burned this entire property to the ground. Just like his mother. Do not revisit those memories upon me."

The young minister shifted with embarrassment. "Of course, my lord. It wasn't my intention." He bowed his head. "My apologies."

Diomedes was tight-lipped for a moment. "If these rumors have reached a point where they may prove to undermine the Empire, I will have to address them. Draft a speech for me, denouncing any speculative ties that the royal family has with Skylok."

"Of course, sir."

"What of our leads on…on its hideout?" the ruler continued. Strangely, the objectification of Skylok seemed to make him uncomfortable. "I was informed that Captain Alrik of Empyrean's Guard had a written report about possible locations for some of the savages' villages. He had suspicions about the coasts near the Lenoran border, as well as Odelwhite Forest."

"Sire. I have the report here." The advisor who'd briefed the leader on the rebellious Katruskik peoples gestured to one of the scrolls in front of him.

"Good, bring it to my study. I'll have a look at it later today. Is that all?"

"It is, Your Highness."

"Well, in that case…" Diomedes stood and rested his hand on the back of his chair. "I call this meeting adjourned. Continue to work well, as you have."

His advisors stood respectfully. "Yes, my lord."

Nodding, Diomedes turned to the balcony that was behind him. Passing by the soldiers who flanked the open-air doorway, he crossed onto the terrace and walked away.

It wasn't long after he'd entered one of the largest parlors of his Estate did he bend over and cough brilliantly into his kerchief again. Succumbing to a short fit, he leaned a hand against one of the painted walls and pressed through until it subsided. When it did at last, he lowered the cloth.

There was blood in it.

He wiped his mouth with a spot of the fabric that wasn't yet stained.

Turning his eyes to one side of the parlor, he found himself facing down a tall statue of Empyrean. The great horned bird had its wings tucked, a rarity for any of its depictions, and its head was lifted regally as it looked over the room. Curtains were tied off on either side of it and at its feet was a sacrificial dish of roasted meat. The sweet herbs that had been used to season the delicacy filled the room and drifted out of the doorway that led into a tiny courtyard, which connected the parlor to another wing of the Estate.

"Please," Diomedes prayed quietly, and he closed his eyes. With his free hand, he clutched at the locket that was hanging around his neck. "Just give me a little more time."

Empyrean answered him with stony silence.

Opening his eyes, Diomedes looked at his locket. He flicked it open gently.

There was a small painting inside, consisting of three faces that were familiar to him: there was his own bust on the right, though he looked younger, and his flinty eyes were staring fixedly ahead; to the left of him was a beautiful Arkanian woman, with light brown skin, burgundy hair that sat atop her shoulders in thick waves and large, penetrating eyes of black; in her arms she carried a golden-eyed babe with sky blue locks and a curious expression.

If his life were normal, and his family history just so, the sight of the painting would have caused him to smile. But now, and every time he dared to look at it, it only brought a dull ache to his heart.

"All those years…and I couldn't find you." With his thumb, Diomedes stroked the infant's round, blushing cheek. "But it's you, isn't it? After all this time, you suddenly returned. And yet…" The skin around his eyes scrunched with despair. "Once again, I must discard you. For your own safety…and that of everyone across this continent."

Of course, the infant's face offered no reaction. Even if Diomedes could actually hold him and speak to him presently, the babe wouldn't have understood.

But, so far as Diomedes knew, this child was a young man now. So his understanding had broadened. And Diomedes suspected that he didn't hold any positive standing in that young man's mind.

He closed his eyes again. "How you must hate me."

"Good afternoon, Princess Adiné."

"Good afternoon," came the addressed royal's reply.

Diomedes' golden eyes snapped up. Shutting the locket, he let it fall against his chest.

His daughter was coming down the hallway as she greeted one of the servants. She stopped in the parlor's doorway, spying his silhouette, and seeing that it was him she crossed into the room with a bit of a bounce in her step. She seemed to be proud of something.

"Adiné," he greeted, turning to her.

"Father," she smiled as she came to him.

Sixteen years of age Princess Adiné was growing into a beautiful young woman, with brown skin and voluminous, burgundy hair that rested on her shoulders in thick waves. Her big, dark eyes were piercing, glinting like onyx, and her dress billowed in her wake. Ankle-length, the sleeveless white-and-magenta gown was cinched at the waist and from the gold rings that secured it over her shoulders folds of silken fabric fell over her arms. When she walked, they fluttered like the wings of a butterfly. Upon her head there was a gilded crown of leaves, of which only the one in the middle was embedded with a dazzling, Lenoran crystal.

"Are you all right?" she asked when she saw the fatigue in his eyes.

"I'm fine," he said, smiling thinly. "I just had another meeting. You know how those can be."

Adiné didn't seem satisfied with his answer.

Diomedes sought to change the subject before she could question him further. "What is it that brings you here? And where's Mattatheus?"

Adiné rolled her eyes. "I don't know." She circled away from him with a careless shrug and sauntered to the center of the room, where an artful floor mosaic depicted a man slaying a multi-headed beast. "And I don't care."

Diomedes couldn't help smiling. "You still don't like him."

"I just don't understand why you're always asking about him," she said, rounding on him. "Why not adopt him and make him your daughter?"

Diomedes chuckled outright. "I only wonder because it's past noon, and the two of you are supposed to be in the library so he can tutor you in politics."

Adiné groaned, her shoulders sagging.

"He's going to be your aide, Adiné," Diomedes reminded her seriously, "for when you take my place. Like it or not the two of you are going to have to get along."

"Maybe if he wasn't so *boring,*" Adiné complained. "I was with him in the library, until I managed to slip away. I may or may not have seen him looking for me in the courtyard, but I don't know if he's still there. I just know that wherever he is now, I am not."

"Adiné…"

"What? He won't notice, he's always got that chiseled face of his stuck in a tome anyway." She sniffed and cleared her throat, not meaning for the compliment to have slipped out. "Eventually he'll return to the library and find me sitting there, reading, and it'll be like I never left."

Diomedes looked at her with an expression that only a father could make.

Adiné wasn't fazed. She folded her arms. "You know, if you keep pushing me to keep my head in a scroll I might come to resent you," she said smartly. "I saw that in a play."

"I'm sure you did." Diomedes couldn't stop another smile from pulling on his lips.

Adiné cocked her head cutely, one eyebrow raised, and she lifted her shoulder briefly.

Diomedes stared at her, no longer a scolding adult but a doting father. His eyes started watering.

She noticed. With her arms falling, she eyed him worriedly. "What's wrong?"

"Nothing." He turned his gaze aside and blinked his tears away. "It's just…you've been reminding me of your mother a lot more these days. She was always making comments like that, telling me that I take work too seriously and have no balance…" He smiled to himself and Adiné saw that it was filled with sorrow.

Her playful disposition faltered for a moment, then faded. She thought for a second. "Have you…ever considered finding a new wife?"

Diomedes turned on her in bewilderment, almost anger. He reined it in with a rapid shake of his head. "No. No one can replace your mother."

"So it seems." Spreading her arms, Adiné spun delicately and leaned against a plinth not far from the middle of the room. Casting her eyes to the painted ceiling, she sighed. "I wish I remembered her." She paused. "And my brother."

Diomedes glanced over at her, but said nothing.

"Sometimes, I wonder what life would've been like if they were here." She pointed her sandaled toes and stretched her hands towards them. "Probably a lot less boring, I bet."

She heard her father chuckle, and she smiled.

"I'm sure…that all we can do is make them proud on this side, until we go to be with them beyond the aether," he said.

"Yes…" Adiné responded distantly. "I suppose that's all."

A space of silence passed between them.

Diomedes cleared his throat. "Right. Now, you've taken a long enough break. I'm sure by now Mattatheus is worried that he'll be hanged for having lost sight of you. Ease his nerves, will you?"

Adiné straightened with a heavy sigh. "Fine…" She started for the doorway. "I'll see you at dinner."

Diomedes nodded in agreement. It wasn't until after she left that he allowed a troubled and guilty frown to cross his face.

Hardly a moment later, hurried panting came to him from behind.

He circled in time to see a servant stumble into the parlor by way of the tiny, neighboring courtyard. Dressed in a simple tunic, belt and sandals, he was carrying a letter.

Its seal was unbroken, but its imperfect state suggested that it had passed through many different hands.

"Y-Your Highness!" Out of breath, the servant bowed swiftly and righted himself just as fast. "I have a message for you! From Viscount Hydeman of Orinn, sire!"

"The viscount?" Diomedes extended his hand, to which the servant responded by surrendering the letter to him. Unfolding it, Diomedes began to read. "What, has Earl Elkiah suddenly decided he's too good to…write…"

He stopped, his golden eyes freezing on the first few lines of the message.

Glancing at the servant, who stood there, waiting, he scanned the rest of the letter quite quickly.

"Sire, I was told to deliver an oral message in tandem," the man told him.

"Yes, what is it?" Diomedes pressed impatiently, his eyes still roving the letter.

"Sire: 'the Shade has entered Lyrik.'"

Diomedes froze. He felt the blood drain from his face.

Carefully he looked up and stared at the messenger, his vibrant eyes wide and unflinching.

The servant swallowed.

At last Diomedes looked away, thinking, his mind running faster than a free-range saiga. "Who gave you this letter?" he inquired, folding it and holding it up referentially.

"Just a messenger, sire." The young man shrugged. "Like me."

"…I see." Diomedes' eyes seemed brighter, far more intense than they normally were as he looked upon the young deliveryman. Again he turned aside, his unblinking gaze an indication of his speeding thoughts. "Thank you. You're dismissed."

"Sire." Bowing, the servant left the way that he'd came.

Behind him, Diomedes looked to the statue of Empyrean once more, helplessly this time.

It seemed he had to fit in another meeting.

✺✺✺

"Behold!" Dillon thrust his fist into the tawny, evening sky. Wearing a half-mask that looked like a golden-eyed, white and blue lion, he was dressed in a stunning costume complete with blue-dyed pants and tassels, as well as a white-and-blue top that looked like the blouse of a foreign royal. A sky-blue ponytail erupted from the mane of his mask, falling nearly to his ankles. A few braids were woven into it, each decorated with golden trinkets. "Now I, Zion, will seal you away! Empyrean! Vedrah!" He dropped his hand and aimed his palm at the two who were standing across from him.

Both were classmates and friends of his from the schoolhouse, though their faces were impossible to discover. For, like Dillon, they were wearing masks — but theirs were oversized and intimidating.

One was that of a basilisk, complete with slitted red eyes and nostrils, as well as a texture of scaly skin that shimmered whenever the wearer turned his head. The other wore a mask that looked like a humanoid version of a ferocious, horned eagle, complete with wings that grew from the back of its head. Both of them, like Dillon, wore flamboyant costumes to match.

Around them, other children who were dressed for theatre were lying on the ground, pretending to be dead soldiers or fallen warriors.

"Prepare yourselves!" Dillon cried.

Off-stage and behind him, Tyre crouched close to the ground and spread his hand in the boy's direction. In the blink of an eye a steady stream of wind erupted from his palm, split around the young star, and crashed into his roleplaying enemies.

At Tyre's back, a trio of villagers with rope-tuned goblet drums began to play a fast, exhilarating rhythm, and they were swiftly joined by someone playing a gourd drum that was covered in a net of round beads. Together, they created a heart-shaking beat of rising anticipation. When a flutist joined in, their song created such an orchestral harmony of suspense that several of the villagers watching the Feast of Liberty production shifted anxiously.

Lilian, who was sitting with Liam in the midst of the watching crowd, grabbed his arm with a squeak.

He shushed her gently and stroked her hair. But he barely turned his attention from the children's play.

"Argh!" the girl dressed as the winged beast, Empyrean, blocked her face with her arms. "Curse you, Zion!"

The boy donning the mask of the basilisk, Vedrah, cried out dramatically, one arm up to guard himself from the unrelenting winds.

Dillon slammed the heels of his hands together and yelled, cuing Tyre to unleash a slightly stronger gale.

He did.

Opposite Tyre, another aetheriest knelt at the edge of the children's invisible stage and caused the earth to jump beneath Empyrean.

She was vaulted over Tyre's jet stream — much to the crowd's delight — and fell towards Zion with an aerial punch.

Zion retreated, signaling for Tyre to rescind his attack, which he promptly did. Dodging his co-star's fist, he and Empyrean transitioned into a round of choreographed sparring.

Vedrah joined in, tipping the odds in his and Empyrean's favor.

"Oh no!" Lilian exclaimed.

"Is it me, or is this way more dramatic than the version that we did?" Brent asked Renée quietly. The two weren't far from Liam and his niece, having secured a bench table with Aaron, Harver and Eklaire not long after the Feast had begun. Brent had both of his arms resting on the table, with one lying behind Renée. "They even changed Zion's costume."

"They put a lot of work into it," Renée whispered back. "You know how exciting it is to act out *The Third Aether War*. It becomes the highlight of any Feast it's done at!"

They watched as the fictional fist-fight raged on with artful kicks and complicated combos.

"Who choreographed this?" Brent frowned.

"Garret and Irma," Renée recalled.

Zion cartwheeled into a jumping spin-kick that knocked Vedrah off his feet.

"I tried that in a fight once," Brent said.

"Did it work?" Renée looked at him curiously.

"Nah, I fell."

"Before you sprang back up and punched that slave trader in the nose."

"Exactly! Wow, it's like you were there!"

Renée giggled.

"Guys, shut up, I'm tryna watch!" Aaron hissed.

Renée and Brent exchanged looks and laughed quietly.

All at once, there was a collective gasp when Zion was overpowered and collapsed. Battle-worn and gasping, he lay on the ground as Empyrean and Vedrah stood over him.

"No, Zion!" a child called out from somewhere in the crowd. Several others chuckled softly, amused by how engaged he was in the story.

Brent wasn't exempt. But his smile slowly faded when, looking beyond the circular stage and into the growing shadows near the village, he noticed something.

A dark figure, cloaked by the smoke that was billowing out of the bonfire; an unruly mane of black hair; a snarling mask with jagged, sharp teeth —

He started, rising partway out of his seat.

"Brent?" Renée looked at him.

The shadows shifted, roiled as the smoke continued to blow across the field.

Brent squinted.

The masked figure was gone.

Or had it been his imagination the entire time?

He wasn't sure. But it left a bad feeling in his stomach.

Applause brought him back to the present. He returned to the play.

Zion had risen and Brent caught the last few blows of the fight before Empyrean and Vedrah fell and moved no more.

"And so, Zion the Hero defeated the evil plaguing the world, and saved the day!" the narrator, Mekial, called out and as another round of applause went up, all of the children from the show — including those who'd pretended to be dead for the final scene or had had earlier roles — came in front of the audience, removed their masks, and bowed collectively.

Though his friends applauded with everyone else, Brent's eyes turned back to the same spot that had caught his attention before.

Still just shifting smoke.

The sides of his eyes flinched, tightened with confusion.

"I liked it a lot!" an Arkanian girl said to Lilian, having found her after the show ended. She was a friend of hers and was close to her age. "It's a fun story!"

"Yeah!" Lilian agreed. "Avats can't use the aether but *The Third Aether War* is about Zion, an Avat who was the most powerful aetherian to ever walk the earth! Then he beat up Empyrean and Vedrah all on his own! And he saved the world!" She threw her arms into the air.

"It's just a story, Lil," Liam reminded her, placing a hand on her head.

"I know, but it's a *cool* story!" she whined, twisting to get a good look at him.

He smiled gently.

"Brent." Renée's voice called him back to the present.

He turned from the fields to look at her.

A frown of concern was picking at her brow. "Is everything okay?"

"Huh? O-oh, yeah. Listen, I'll be right back. Save me some dessert!" He touched her shoulder as he skirted around her. Weaving through the crowd of villagers, some of whom were filing towards the buffet table or were going to congratulate the children on their show, he jogged back towards the village.

"Where's he going?" Aaron asked, sucking the last bit of meat off of a small animal bone. "He's gonna miss the graduation."

"Maybe he had to go tinkle?" Eklaire offered.

Neither Aaron nor Renée responded to that. But Renée did cast a concerned look in Brent's direction as he ran further from the Feast and back towards Taranis.

49

THE FURTHER BRENT got from Taranis' yearly celebration, which was being held farther out in the valley due to the village's growing size, the quieter it became. Soon, the jumble of voices was nothing more than white noise in his ears.

When he got to the farmlands, he slowed to a stop and glanced around the field.

He was sure that he'd seen the masked man here somewhere. It couldn't have possibly been a trick of his own mind.

Could it?

Something caught his eye only just up the hill. Fixing his eyes upon it, he was surprised to learn that it was the very same man that he was looking for.

Or it was the last glimpse of him at least: he was rounding a corner and venturing deeper into the village.

Without a moment's thought, Brent went after him.

But when he twisted around that same corner, he had to stop before he crashed into a young couple.

"Sorry," he muttered, stepping out of their way.

They forgave him, thinking little of the accident, and as they ambled back to the party Brent searched the road.

There was no one else around. There weren't even footprints to hint at where the masked figure had gone.

His golden eyes wandered about, his brow furrowing, before his gaze doubled back to the crown of the hill.

The stranger was there, vanishing behind the chief's house this time.

"Hey!" Brent shouted and he darted up the hill after him.

As he hiked up the incline he found himself wishing he had his bladed staffs with him. Even if today was a celebration, it was careless of him to go somewhere without them.

Breaking around the bend, he searched the area.

Again, nothing.

Again a shadow: there, circling the Main House to enter the wood behind it.

Brent kicked into another sprint.

With the sun setting behind the hills, the woods were getting dark. So he tread carefully, his ears so sharply attuned to the sighs of the forest that they practically buzzed. Turning this way and that, he searched for any sign of the intruder that he'd spotted. He scanned the silhouettes of birches, the frame of boughs, studied the shiver of a bush.

But, there was nothing.

At last, he stopped in a tiny clearing that he knew to be the halfway point between Taranis and the amari tree. He spun around.

His heart jumped.

There the masked man was again, at the end of the forest, just about to walk behind the thick trunk of a tree.

Biting back a call for him to wait — for at this point Brent believed that he surely wouldn't — he darted through the trees and leaped out of the wood after him.

But by the time he got there, the man was gone.

"Wh…" He stepped farther into the open, tossing his eyes to and fro. "What the…"

He was now at the bottom of the hill that led to the amari tree. Glancing this way and that he searched high and low for the shadow that he'd followed, but there was no sign of him anywhere. It wasn't until his eyes rolled towards the shivering vines of the amari tree did he choose to temporarily abandon his hunt.

Treading quietly, he ascended the hill and paused before Adelle's headstone. Pink petals were descending upon it.

Kneeling down, he brushed them off of the grave and rested his hand upon it. With his thumb, he traced her name.

Hardly a second later his face fell and his ears prickled, catching voices.

He looked over his shoulder, towards the western fields. Rising, he followed the murmuring tones to the edge of the cliff and looked down into the plains.

Immediately, he dropped to the ground with his belly in the grass.

Xëri was in the field below.

And she was talking to a man in a half-mask.

The significance of that day immediately vacated Brent's mind, with the jubilant feast that celebrated Taranis' birth, the chief's speech and the graduation of the auction raid trainees. Indeed, at that very moment, villagers were settling in their seats while the chief rose to deliver his oration.

Only one of the villagers peeked in Taranis' direction — Renée — and she searched the edge of the village for any sign of Brent's return. But there was none.

Her disappointment was clear.

But Brent was unaware, for his thoughts were full of questions that were aimed at Xëri and the masked stranger. Creeping forward, he peeked over the cusp of the hill to see them again.

The masked stranger was gone, and Xëri was making her way back to the hill.

The absence of the mysterious visitor confused him for a second. But he hurriedly scrambled backwards and got to his feet. Glancing about, he searched for something that could explain his being where he was.*tv*

At length, Xëri appeared over the rise of the path. She lifted her eyebrows at the sight of him.

Brent turned, casually at that, trying to seem as if he'd been visiting Adelle's grave the entire time.

"Brent?" She cocked her head. "What're you doing out here? Don't tell me the Feast is over already. It's not even nightfall."

"I…" He composed himself. "I came up to the house looking for something and got a little distracted."

SECRETS OF TARANIS
CODE: GRADUATION

"Oh…" Xëri cast a sad look between him and Adelle's grave.

His eyes flitted between her and the headstone before he continued. "What're you doing up here?"

She took a deep breath and raised her shoulders. "I just needed to take a bit of a break from so many people!" She smiled. "It's not easy being second-in-command of Taranis."

"Oh…" Brent nodded absently. "Well" — he flicked his chin to the valley — "were you talking to someone just now?"

Her eyebrows twitched and she gave him a funny look. "No, I was by myself," she told him and she glanced out into the valley to see if there was someone she hadn't noticed.

There wasn't.

"But…" Brent peeked into the field with her and then away, thinking.

Had he been seeing things?

Or was she simply lying again?

Xëri's own eyes flinched with a tiny smile. "You've gone on a couple of missions back-to-back only a few days ago, and you haven't been able to get as much sleep," she reminded him. "Believe it or not, it's possible for even the best of our raiders to get jittery when they're not off fighting for their lives somewhere. Maybe you should head back to the Feast and try to wind down a little. Being with Aaron and the others should help you calm down."

"Right…" He looked up feebly. "Probably. You gonna come?"

"In a minute." She smiled tightly. "I think I might pay my respects before I go."

"Oh. Right." He stepped aside to look at Adelle's grave. "Guess I'll leave you to it."

Xëri nodded warmly.

He returned the gesture. But he soon frowned at something over her shoulder.

There was nothing there though, besides the slope of the cliff as it angled downward into the valley. Still, he couldn't shake the strangest feeling that something was watching him from that direction.

Noticing his wandering eyes, Xëri tilted her head at him. "Brent?"

He looked at her sharply.

"Are you all right?"

"Yeah." Blinking, he shook his head and forced a quick smile. "It's just…you're right." He puckered his brow. "Maybe I'm just a little wound up."

With her own forehead creasing, Xëri parted her lips as if to say something, but nothing came out.

"I'll head back first." He started away. "See you."

"Until later." She smiled.

He bobbed his chin and with one final, dubious glance over her shoulder, he walked away. It was only when his back was to her did a dark shadow cross over his brow.

Sleep-deprived or not, he trusted his instincts. And at that moment, they were telling him that he hadn't been hallucinating.

As far as masked men went…Xëri knew something.

But he continued to feign ignorance, dipping himself deeper into the shadows of the trees as he made his way back to Taranis and to the celebration.

Without a word, Xëri watched him leave.

When she could no longer hear his footsteps with her pointed ears, she sighed and turned around.

No sooner had she done so did the man that she was speaking to earlier reappear behind her, transparently at first, until he was just as solid and real as she was.

Dressed from head to toe in black, he wore a half-mask that was a cross between a lion and a dicanus. Rivers of straight, silky hair mixed with jeweled braids hung down his back, falling from the mask's crown, and the plated armor on his shoulders caught the sunlight.

"Qavë ya ovë mi qizhuiwa," he said to her.

Xëri understood immediately: *"He noticed me."*

"But…he's not an aetheriest," she said, turning to him.

"No," Oruviçu agreed. "But I won't deny that he certainly sensed me."

Xëri frowned and her eyes drifted away in consideration. "Then I suppose it's a good thing that you warned me when you did. I didn't even notice him on the hill until you said something."

Oruviçu observed her, considering. "You're out of practice."

Xëri rounded on him, almost hurt. She lowered her eyes in disappointment. "That…can't be helped," she said, though the tone of her voice suggested guilt. "You know what I agreed to."

Oruviçu didn't offer a response to that. But, turning, he did gaze in the direction that Brent had gone. He was still for a long while.

A second later the touch of his quintessence entered the air, its presence so heavy that Xëri was almost certain she could've reached out and grabbed it.

Deep in the woods, where he'd chosen to hide behind a gathering of shrubs, Brent felt a chill race down his spine. He barely had the chance to blink before something collided with his gut, blowing the air clean out of him. Swallowing a grunt, he doubled over and clutched his stomach. His head spun and the world seemed to teeter all around him.

He cursed silently. Then, gritting his teeth, he ducked out of the bushes and retreated.

Hearing his departure, Oruviçu withdrew his quintessence from the currents of the aether.

"Don't worry," he said suddenly, for he soon noticed Xëri's unease. "I didn't do much. But, he will be sore in the morning."

Though still troubled, Xëri seemed to calm at his assurance.

"False pretenses…and a false faith." Oruviçu looked into the woods again, as if he could still see Brent's distancing shape. "Imperial Avats are strange, believing that they can no longer link themselves to the aether. Though, I do understand." He faced her. "Their ignorance is not your fault. You've kept up your charade for their sake. As well as ours."

Xëri held her tongue, but the muted distress in her dark eyes spoke for her.

"…I apologize." Oruviçu's sincerity caused her to look up. "I hadn't considered how hard this would be for you."

"No." She shook her head. "It was my decision. You couldn't have done anything about it."

Oruviçu watched her, but he didn't press the subject.

"Xëri," he started, "the boy's bloodline is manifesting."

She turned her eyes to him.

"Slowly, but surely." He faced her completely. "Given his heritage, and his ability to discern that I was here…it can't be denied. He's a lot like Çaru'qu's last chosen. Perhaps that is why he still hasn't made his move yet. Though, his timing has never been something that any mortal has ever been able to understand."

The truth of Oruviçu's words weren't lost on Xëri. "Still, either way, it's happening again," she said gravely. "Their return. Çaru'qu would've remained silent otherwise."

"The danger draws near, yes," he agreed. "And the signs are obvious: Brusseir grows ever more restless, and the other Shades of the Order have shared news of strange happenings in the Empire: the increased demand for blood sacrifices being among them, as well as rumors of a military elixir birthed from the imperial capital. Even I fear what it may be capable of, and of what we will find ourselves to be a part of when it is distributed."

Xëri pursed her lips tightly and her eyes wandered away.

"The duties of rescuing the slaves will only occupy you for so long," Oruviçu told her and he took a few steps away from her, creating space. "But the pieces are falling into place, and we of the Order are well aware of what that means for us. I only hope that you will soon come to realize the same."

"I'm surprised." Xëri smiled fleetingly. "You haven't tried to tell me that Brent is dangerous, and that his being here will make all of this far more complicated."

"No," Oruviçu said. "I've already come to realize that such words have no affect on you, when they are coming from someone like me."

Xëri pressed her lips tightly.

"But I will say this: that boy carries fate in his hands. And no matter how one sees him…that is what makes him more dangerous than any threat looming over us."

Xëri lowered her eyes, considering that.

Oruviçu didn't say anything more. Soon, a sudden stillness overtook the air.

Xëri raised her head.

Oruviçu was gone.

When Brent returned to the Feast, he slinked along the edge of the tabled crowds and slipped into an open spot beside Aaron. He moved carefully, for he was still in pain from the aetherial force that had struck him.

Ivan was speaking in front of the bonfire, but as far as what the topic was Brent wasn't paying attention.

"Aaron." Keeping his voice quiet, he dropped back into his seat.

The redhead wheeled on him and did a double-take. His voice came out as a hiss. "What the —?"

"I need to talk to you."

"Where did you go —?!"

Suddenly, the entire gathering of villagers erupted into applause. The two looked up.

It was then that Brent saw Ivan standing in front of the bonfire. Renée was next to him, along with all of the other trainees who were graduating into the ranks of the slave auction raiders.

Shoulders straight and her chin lifted, she looked out over the cheering audience with glimmering, dark eyes.

It wasn't long before she made eye contact with her mother, who lifted her wooden mug in solidarity.

Next to the woman, Ben whistled with his fingers in his mouth, cheered and applauded.

"That's my girl!" he shouted over everyone's ring of support.

Mekial was just as enthusiastic. Jumping with one fist punching the sky, he applauded his sister with a bright grin. Some of his friends were with him, cheering in the same way. All were still wearing their costumes from the play.

Spreading his arms to quell the excitement, Ivan called for dessert. Slowly the applause faded, villagers filed away for the conclusive sweets, and the newly inducted raiders were allowed to disperse and rejoin their loved ones.

"Way to blow off Ren's graduation," Aaron grunted, frowning at Brent. Truly, his face was far more suspicious than it was disapproving.

Brent didn't notice, for he was far too busy looking over the mingling crowd in quiet surprise. He soon spotted Renée going to her family.

Eklaire, Harver and Liam joined them to offer their congratulations, as did Tyre and Kro. A few others did so in passing.

"Where did you go?" Aaron demanded again. "Don't tell me you actually had to go to the outhouse."

Brent turned on him, frowning. "Outhouse? No."

"Hmph. Well, after you took off to wherever, Ren kept checking to see if you were coming back. Then Dad called her up."

"She…" That gave Brent pause. "She did?"

He looked over at Renée again.

She was laughing and smiling between their friends, grateful for their support.

His face softened. But, disappointed in himself, a frown quickly took him and he looked away from her.

Aaron rolled his eyes and got up. "I'm gonna go talk to her. Wait." He stopped. "You said you needed something."

"What? Oh." Brent shook his head. "It's nothing. I'll tell you later."

He got out of his seat, too. But when Aaron went to give Renée his good wishes, Brent lingered.

He didn't make his way to her until she was mostly alone, or at least as alone as one could be while waiting in line for dessert at a buffet table.

Keeping out of her peripheral vision, he came up behind her and leaned towards her.

"Congrats," he said and he straightened up just as she circled around.

"Oh." Her glow faded and his heart sank. "Thanks…" For a moment her eyes were low and her brow puckered in growing confusion. She looked at him again. "Where did you go? Earlier, just after the play. It seemed urgent."

"Oh, that." Brent scratched the back of his head, his gaze inching aside. "It wasn't anything, really. Just…thought I lost something, and had to go find it."

Renée studied him, from his awkward air to how he wouldn't

look her in the eye. "Well…did you find it?"

"Uh." They moved up in line. "Not really."

"Not really?"

"I mean…sort of."

"Hm." Renée faced away and fell quiet.

Brent took a breath. "Um, Ren, I…"

She looked at him.

"I'm sorry." He was sincere. "I know I missed your ceremony."

"…It's okay." Renée shook her head and smiled fleetingly at him. "I'm sure whatever it was, you didn't think you'd be gone that long."

She moved forward in line, and Brent loitered for a second before stepping up to her again. "I just, know how much it meant to you," he said. "What with everything you had to do to get there —"

"Then how come you left?" Renée turned on him and while her outburst gave vent to her anger, it wasn't at all consuming her. The look in her eyes was more imploring than that. "I just…" She sighed. "My mom, my dad…Liam, Aaron, Jeffrey…everyone who I felt played a huge role in my becoming a raider was there to see it. To see Chief Ivan officiate me in front of everyone. I just…wish you'd been there, too."

She didn't say anything else. Taking another step in line she scooped some candied yams into the wooden bowl she was carrying and walked away.

Brent hesitated only for a second before he went after her. "Ren. Hey, Ren." Catching her by the shoulder, he gently turned her towards him.

Though she was waiting for him to say something, there was nothing in her face to suggest she was keen on hearing it.

"I'm sorry," he said again, his hand falling from her. "This was something that you worked really hard for and I bailed for…" He ruffled his hair. "Something stupid at the last second."

Renée shifted her weight, looking like she wanted to walk away.

Brent noticed. "But, hey, that doesn't mean I don't still support you," he told her. "I missed your ceremony, but you can bet I'll be there when you punch your first slave trader in the nose. I'll make sure to have Pops put you on our team for your first mission."

Renée considered the offer. She smiled softly. "Okay."

He smiled back. "Oh — and I *do* have something for you by the way." Reaching back, he pulled something out of the folds of one of his sashes and held it out to her.

It was a figurine made of a mesmerizing white-and-mint-colored stone, and it was shaped like a warrior who lifted their sword in a stance of battle. Judging by the curve of its body, it was distinctly female. The blade, glinting like metal in the sunlight, was reminiscent of the sword that Renée had come to use as her principle weapon.

Plucking the object from his grasp, which was the length of her hand, she studied it from all angles. The workmanship was awkward in some places, but the overall image was clearly depicted. What made it even more impressive was the way it caught the sunset, filtering the crimsons of the sky through its rounded, green planes. The result was a mottled collection of colorful lights that danced across her hand. At times, it even made the statuette look like it was moving.

"I found that gemstone in Heletia a while back," Brent told her. "Aaron actually gave me some pointers on how to cut it. I figured you could put it in your room somewhere, y'know, to memorialize today. Maybe by your window, or something."

"Is this…supposed to be me?" she finally asked, tearing her eyes from the statuette to look at him.

Brent felt his cheeks get hot. "Well…yeah. I mean, I was thinking of you when I made it, so I —" He broke off suddenly when she hugged him.

His face felt like a furnace. Not to say that he was bothered by her touch. In fact, he rather liked it.

"Thanks, Brent," she said, letting him go, and she smiled at his gift. "I love it."

Still blushing hard, his face lit up with hope. "You do?"

She nodded.

As if on cue Eklaire walked by, wearing Dillon's elaborate mask from the play.

"Aww, lookit ya'll!" she teased.

Renée shyly brushed her hair behind her ear.

"Shut up," Brent said in a way to hide his own embarrassment.

Lifting the mask Eklaire winked at Renée, who laughed as if to brush aside her friend's suggestion.

She didn't notice Brent's eyes fall to her in that same moment, his gaze as soft as her own smile.

The rest of the celebration was a satisfying event, with several impromptu performances, spirited conversations and plenty of laughter. Towards the end of the night children played by the river and volunteers began cleaning up, ferrying tables away and gathering dishes for storage.

Brent assisted by partnering with several other men to store the bench tables in a shed at the lower end of the village. It wasn't long before the final table was loaded into the building, whereupon Brent took it upon himself to lock the place up.

He shared goodbyes with the others, who ventured off to find their own friends and family. As they departed, Brent looked towards the field where still more people were assisting with the breakdown.

Xëri was there, calling out instructions as she helped to gather dishes.

Something like a scowl must've passed over his face, for the next thing he knew Aaron had appeared at his side and addressed it.

"What's wrong?" He followed Brent's line of sight. "Why d'you keep glaring at Mom like that?"

Brent cast him a fleeting glance and proceeded to close the storage doors. After that, he locked them. "I saw her behind the village earlier," he said. "She was talking to someone: a guy in a mask."

Aaron's eyes grew, stunned. "Like the guy you saw in Cleopa?"

"Yeah. Didn't look like the same one, though."

Aaron turned on his mother. Slowly his surprise waned and a look of steel took its place. "So then…Mom knows something about them, too."

"Yeah." Brent watched Xëri as she started towards Taranis alongside a pair of other women, dishes in arm. "Looks that way."

Murdoch swallowed roughly. Stiff as a boulder, he kept his head low as he knelt in the audience chamber of the emperor.

A cavernous room of deep scarlets and meticulously patterned walls, the audience hall was supported by looming red columns that were evenly spaced throughout. On the right, an open balcony allowed twilight to dance inside — a warm glow that saturated the area and yet, it couldn't cast out the strange cold that chilled Murdoch down to his very bones. If he ever did dare to squint in the light's direction, he was sure he'd be able to see the entirety of the labyrinthine palace, with its many cusped gates and gables, nourished gardens, manmade lakes and island pavilions.

But he dared not look, for he was far too intimidated by the presence of the man who sat in the elaborately sculpted throne at the head of the room. Only his guards and the crown that he wore — one of gilded leaves and eagle wings — caught the dying light of day. Everything else about the imperial leader was ensnared in shadow, for no lowly citizen from outside the palace had ever laid eyes on the one who ruled over them.

But his very presence was suffocating, icy. Indeed, it was the source of the cold that swept down Murdoch's spine, freezing the trickles of sweat that were there until he shook.

He gulped again and it hurt.

He'd buttoned his collar too tight.

"Murdoch." When the emperor finally addressed him out of the darkness, Murdoch jumped. The man's voice was smooth, oily. It unnerved his guest. "That was your name, wasn't it?"

"Y-yes, Your Highness," the slave trader stammered. His breath felt short.

He'd been summoned to the emperor's palace at least two weeks ago, several days after he and his team had been ambushed between the walls of Heletica's Pass. Although his wife Marianne and their daughter had done their best to encourage him through their letters after learning the news, for he'd been summoned right after the holiday caravan's travels and so had had no opportunity to go home, he couldn't help but feel anxious. He didn't even know what the emperor wanted.

But, despite what Marianne had said, he didn't think it had

anything to do with being promoted.

"I've heard rumors over the past year, Murdoch," the shadowy emperor continued. "Rumors that, I believe, you might be able to shed some light on. Rest assured, whatever answer that you give will not bring harm to you, nor to your family."

Murdoch swallowed again. "I-I'm grateful, milord. A-a-al-though, I'm not sure what information a simple man like me could offer you. I'm just a slave trader, after all. Merchants tend to know even more than we do and —"

"Quiet."

Murdoch clamped his mouth shut. He could feel beads of sweat gliding down the side of his face.

"Hmm." Koberius rested his elbow on the arm of his throne, from which the great wings of an eagle expanded out of the back while the armrests resembled sneering sea serpents. He rested his cheek against his fingers. "Tell me, Murdoch: does the name 'Sky-lok' mean anything to you?"

"S-Sire." Murdoch stared at one spot on the floor. "It's the name of the devil-barbarian that the slave traders of Lyrik Province have released an arrest warrant for. It's been a high-profile criminal for the past year, sir. According to my briefings, anyway. I haven't lived in Lyrik Province for over seven years now, so all I know about it is mostly hearsay."

"Hm. Well, has hearsay at all mentioned to you that there seems to be speculation that this devil is connected to the royal family?"

"I…" Murdoch trailed off. "I believe I may have heard such rumors, Your Majesty, yes."

Koberius watched him carefully. "Certainly an unsightly ru-mor."

"M-Majesty."

"But it intrigued me. So I had my administrators look into the issue and something was brought to my attention: that you, Mur-doch, had come across this devil personally before. Or perhaps, a similar one. Almost seven years ago, you filed a report about a certain goblin that you encountered while working under a Captain Alrik Abronius in the Province of Lyrik."

"Y-yes, Your Majesty," Murdoch responded quickly, bowing

his head towards the floor again, for he'd absently glanced up and spotted the emperor in his throne. The folds of his immaculate robes and draping tunic descended perfectly around his lean frame, and by the fading daylight Murdoch had glimpsed strands of indigo-blue hair before he looked down again.

"I've studied your records extensively, Murdoch," the emperor told him. He lifted his head to look down at the man and his golden eyes were caught by the sunset. "You've served the Empire of Arkania as a slave merchant for most of your adult life. You're dedicated. Loyal. Honest."

"Y-y-you flatter me, Your Majesty." Even though the emperor couldn't see it, Murdoch hastily dropped the foolish grin off of his own face.

Koberius didn't respond to the slave trader's remark. "Your report," he continued, "describes some similarities that seem to exist between the devil you saw seven years ago and Skylok. So imagine my surprise upon learning that one of the last slave traders to have interacted with Skylok is also the same man who drafted this uncanny report? I simply had to meet you and confirm it all for myself."

Murdoch could hear a chilling smile in the young man's voice. He swallowed yet again and for some reason felt a pang of disappointment. Even though he'd already known it, he was a little disheartened to learn that the emperor's summoning really had nothing to do with a promotion. "M-my lord."

"So, Murdoch, I must ask you this next because, being confined to the walls of the palace, I'm unable to determine certain things for myself. But from what I hear it's believed that this devil, this… Skylok, has blue hair. Much like the devil from your report. Is this true?"

"Y-yes, Your Highness. That's true. I saw it with my own eyes. I-i-in fact…and, perhaps it's my own memory playing tricks on me, but, I'm almost certain that Skylok is the same devil from my report, Your Highness. So far as I know, blue hair can't even be found in Lenora…I'm sure it was the same one."

Koberius' eyes narrowed threateningly and his lips thinned into a straight line. His hands were so tense that the bones were visible through his skin when he clutched his armrests. "It would seem, Murdoch…that you and I are the same, in a way."

"S-Sire?"

"Years ago I, too, encountered a devil with blue hair and golden eyes. I had just claimed the throne…and it was a child, whose father had dared to hide its existence from me." Koberius stood, and the motion was so graceful that the folds of his tunic and wrappings shifted around him like streams of silken water.

Murdoch swallowed so hard it was as if he'd eaten a rock.

Koberius lowered his chin to peer down at him. "So I have just one more question for you, Murdoch Macrinus of Northern Lenora."

"S-Sire." For a reason Murdoch couldn't quite place, he dared to lift his head once more.

His heart stopped.

From the shadows where the emperor stood a pair of gleaming, golden eyes were peering right back at him. It was as if he was being pinned by the horrible glare of an insatiable beast.

Murdoch gulped again, and now that he was looking at the throne he noticed that a strange figure was standing just behind the emperor's right shoulder, ghost-like thanks to the way the shadows clung to them from the waist down. A studious glance revealed that the silhouette was that of a woman, but as for her exact features they were just as obscured as the emperor's, bathed in the darkness that was cast by her wide hood.

But even with her face absent to his gaze, Murdoch could feel her stare boring into him as intensely as that of the emperor. It was as if she willed to cleave him in half with it.

And if he wasn't mistaken, her eyes were little more than two scarlet gems sitting in the hollows of her face.

One of the palace guards standing next to him forced his head down, and he saw no more.

"If you were to take your best guess," Koberius continued darkly, and Murdoch suddenly found it harder to breathe; the air in the room felt like it was being compressed from above, as if something was gradually sitting on top of it, "would you claim this devil to look anything like Lyrik's provincial ruler, Viceroy Diomedes?"

"You want to spy on Lady Xëri." Liam was deadpan, his arms folded as he leaned against Greta's hut. Lilian had already been tucked in, and Greta herself had turned in for the night as well. As for the rest of the villagers they, too, had returned to their abodes.

"When you put it that way, you make us sound like creeps," Aaron said, frowning irritably.

"Because it is creepy." Liam straightened. "She's the chief's wife. In case you forgot."

"Of course I didn't!"

Liam grunted.

"We're not spying on her," Brent said. "We're keeping tabs on her until she lets slip some intel about the Elder's daughter, or even about those creeps in masks."

"What difference does that make exactly?"

"Point is, we need intel," Aaron interjected before Brent could retort. "We all know that there's something up with these masked weirdos, not to mention Brent's visions, or whatever. Mom and Dad know something about all of it," his frown loosened with pensive consideration, "and it ties in with this 'Elder' who helped build the Liberation Fronts. But whatever the details are, neither of them are gonna just up and tell us."

"There's gotta be a way we can pull some info out of them…" Crossing his arms and touching his chin, Brent scowled off at nothing.

"…Elder Qëmzhi."

Brent and Aaron looked at Liam, who leaned against the hut again and folded his arms once more.

"He's a good friend of Greta's," Liam continued, "and he helped Laura and I a lot when we first got here. If I'm remembering right, he's been around since the Liberation Fronts got started. On that, he might know something."

"He was one of the first members of the head council," Aaron recalled. "And the first and only one to retire. He's probably got plenty to share."

"Only problem is that the old man's practically senile," Brent reminded them. "We'd be lucky if he even remembers his own name."

"Only when Khirsta's medicine starts to wear off," Liam said. "Talk to him before that, and you might get somethin' out of him. Only lasts for one day at a time, though."

Brent considered this for a second, his blue eyebrows knotting. "Then I guess we'd better make that one day count."

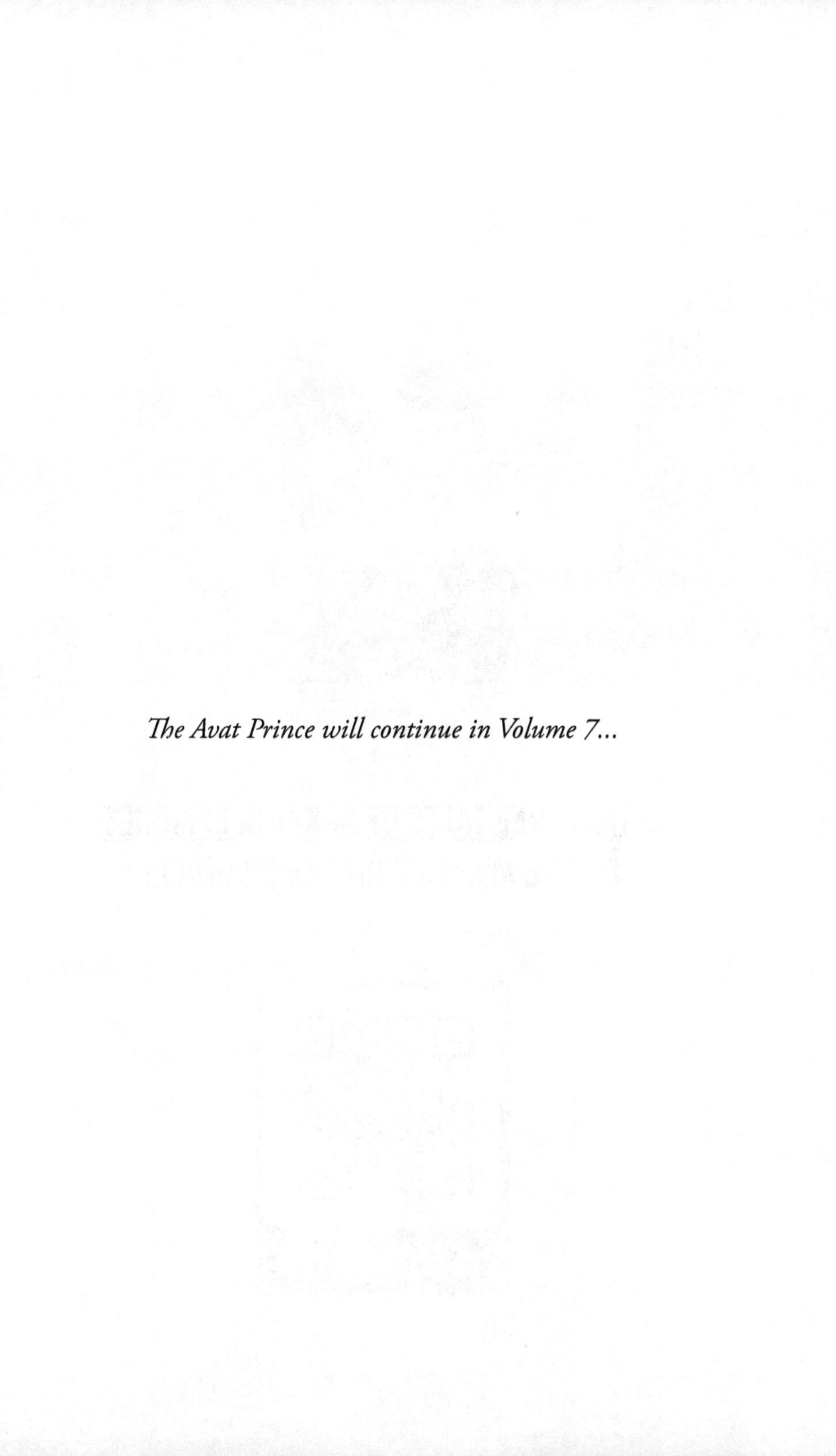

The Avat Prince will continue in Volume 7…

WATCH <u>FREE TALES OF ARKANIA EPISODES</u> ON THE MVP TV YOUTUBE CHANNEL!

NEW THRILLS. NEW TALES.

Brand-new bonus content for *The Avat Prince* every third Saturday!

Featuring an international cast of voice talent, including award-winning VA Josh Portillo!

THE AVAT PRINCE: VOLUME 7

REPORTS SUGGEST THAT the savages and devils who terrorize the Empire are located in these woods," the man answered. "We're here to eradicate them."

Kro's façade nearly slipped. "Eradicate?"

Behind him, Lacey screamed.

He whirled. "Lacey —!"

In the exact same moment, the guardsman who'd stumbled upon the children noticed Lacey's ears, as well as the unquestionable attire that she and the other children were wearing beneath their haphazard disguises.

"Hey!" he hollered to the man Kro was speaking with. "I found some goblins and savages! They're here!"

"You know what to do," said the other.

"Sir!" His subordinate drew his blade.

Kro's eyes sharpened into daggers and he joined the aether. Hardening his stance, he flexed his arms and twisted at the hip.

Before the children's eyes, the ground beneath the guardsman sank and spun him in an isolated circle. Then, it fired him into the air like a springboard.

Before the other imperial could react to what he'd done Kro waved his arms, calling up a tree root.

The creaking branch coiled into the air and surrounded the imperial like a basilisk. Winding itself back, it hurled him through the canopy and out of sight.

"You guys okay?!" Kro shouted up at the children, dropping his stance.

"Yeah, we're good!" Dillon called back, poking his head into Kro's view. "Thank you!"

Kro's urgent expression softened with relief.

"Over here!"

Kro turned, his cloak flapping loudly.

A guardsman had returned. Clearly, he'd seen what had happened.

"Savages!" he shouted, likely to alert any other guardsmen in the area. "They're over here!"

He changed his footing and within seconds, the aether touched Kro's skin.

But it was more apparent than what he was used to.

Eyes growing in understanding, Kro spread his own feet.

A blast of wind erupted around him, and the same green-blue light that the children had witnessed before descended around his body. *"Get down!"* he roared.

Dillon ducked out of view, and he and his friends huddled together.

The imperial aetheriest lifted his hand.

Responding to his influence the aether granted him a flame that danced wildly, shone brightly. Once it had reached the size that the imperial wanted, he sent it surging in Kro's direction.

With a violent roar the fire blazed towards the villager, bombing through trees and bushes like a radioactive missile.

Kro stretched his hands out and a blast of mist left them. It swirled upward quickly, curving around him like an apparition before it hardened into a clear wall of protection.

Howling terribly, the flames slammed into it like an avalanche.

Fire went everywhere and Kro cried out, his arms and knees buckling. Cracks splintered through his barrier like knotted spiderwebs.

"Kro!" Mekial yelled, his hair swaying in the hot air.

Kro winced, his arms shaking. Through the fires that danced outside of his shield, he watched as the imperial aetheriest stretched out his hand again.

This time the fire that he made remained close to his fingers, enveloping them. Gradually they encircled his hand, his wrist, his arm, and then they moved to encase his entire body.

Kro's eyes grew large and his stomach dropped. When he spoke, his voice was hardly louder than the roaring fires and crackling timber. "No way."

"Kro!" Mekial hollered again. "Are you okay?!"

"Mekial!" Kro shouted warningly —

— the imperial aetheriest was completely hidden by a wall of flames now, and the fire was growing fast —

"RUN!"

CONTINUE READING IN
THE AVAT PRINCE: VOLUME 7!

About the Author(ess)

Myranda V. Peterson

A young artist who wears many hats, Myranda Victoria Peterson is an author, illustrator, animator and voice director with a contagious passion for storytelling. She first started off writing plays, which her parents and friends helped her perform when she was a little girl. A self-taught artist, her creative work is heavily inspired by anime and Japanese pop culture. She creates original, high-fantasy content that aims to inspire the youth of today with themes of generosity, courage, friendship and hope.

Myranda is the founder and CEO of the independent imprint and joint animation studio House MVP and lives in Boston, where many famous, classic authors have gone before her. She hopes that one day, her name will join them!